Hidden Scars

Amanda Sue King

Hidden Scars

Visit Amanda King at www.amandasueking.com

Cover Design by Alexandre Rito of Design Project
www.designbookcover.pt/en/

Edited by Brilliant Cut Editing http://brilliantcutediting.blogspot.com

Interior Design and Formatting by Polgarus Studio
www.polgarusstudio.com

Scripture within the text is taken from the King James Version

To Rebecca
Happy reading.
Amanda Dur King
AKA Mandy Hawkins

To my husband
Always

Hope you enjoy the book.
Keep smiling pretty girl.
Ron & Mandy

Prologue

Dad's expression spoke volumes—lips pressed tight, eyes narrowed, nostrils flared. He reminded me of a volcano ready to blow.

"Get out, Morgan," his words spewed forth, thick with venom.

My heartbeat leapt into my throat as I obediently scrambled to leave the bedroom my older sister Marsha and I shared. A wave of nausea rolled over me after I escaped into the hall. *God, please don't let Marsha say anything to provoke him further.*

The door slammed. Then popped back open, leaving just enough space for me to press my right eye to and scan most of the room.

I heard my sister's voice, "You want to fight, then you'll have to fight me like a man."

Dad's cursing and threats intensified. Marsha's voice matched his in volume. Blood raced through my veins. I wanted to run, cover my ears, block out reality, but concern for my seventeen-year-old sister wouldn't allow it.

I choked down an anguished cry as Marsha landed across the bed. She jumped back up and whirled toward him with her fist clenched. He threw her onto the bed again. The metal end of his belt dangled from his right hand, but Marsha refused to lie and wait for the promised beating. Grabbing her by the hair, Dad tossed her to the floor.

Tears streamed down my face as she used the bedpost to pull herself to her feet. I glanced past her, to my mom. She stood against the wall with her arms folded, the always-present instigator of every act of punishment.

A thud snapped my gaze to Marsha. She rubbed the back of her head, her face contorted.

Dad snatched her off her feet and threw her against the wall. Her legs buckled. She slid down the wall. Then as though finding the most remarkable strength, she pushed herself off the floor and stood in front of him, braced and ready to fight.

She pointed to her face. "Hit me."

His eyes narrowed, and his jaw jutted out. He gnawed at his lower lip before grabbing a fistful of blouse and shoving her against the wall again.

"Stop it!" A voice screamed. An unfamiliar voice. Mine. I rushed in the room as if thrust by an unknown force. I'd never stood up to my parents, never talked back, and never raised my voice. "Let go of my sister."

Dad lowered his hands and turned toward me.

With a strength I'd never known, I pushed him away from Marsha.

He fell heavily against the louvered closet doors. They collapsed inward as he lost his balance and landed inside. As if in slow motion, Dad got to his feet. He grabbed me and threw me out of the room. The door banged shut, muffling their screams and scuffles. Pulling my knees to my chest, I tucked my head into my arms and begged, "Please, don't let him hurt her any more. Please, God, help my sister."

The door jerked open, and Dad walked past me, Mom close on

his heels. I hurried to the room and found Marsha sweating, tugging at her ripped shirt. Shaking all over, I asked, "Are you okay?"

She rattled off a string of profanity then took a deep breath. "No, I'm not okay. But now he knows I'm through being his whipping post. If he ever lays a hand on me again, he'll have to hit me where it'll show. Then everybody in this Podunk Mississippi town will see and know about our father, the good deacon. If you've got any sense at all, you'll do the same."

"I'm not like you," my voice quivered.

She held me by the shoulders and drew so close a mist of saliva sprinkled my face. "Then you better change, because no one is going to save you—not our big brother, who I'm sure has busied himself doing something in hopes of escaping their wrath. Not even God."

I never knew what triggered that particular event. My brother, my sister, and I seldom understood what set our parents off. We lived our life waiting, dreading, wondering which one of us would be next. One thing I knew for sure though. My life wasn't going to get any easier in the coming years.

Chapter 1

Bright sunshine streamed through the bedroom window, its warmth welcoming me to the day I'd longed for…prayed for. All was quiet. Too quiet. I lingered in bed and listen. Nothing. Only the constant tick of the bedside clock. Seven thirty. Too early for Mom to have left for work. I tossed the covers, tiptoed to the family room, and checked under the carport. Neither Dad's truck, nor Mom's new 1968 Buick, was there. To be sure, I peeked into their bedroom. The bed was made, the light off. They were gone.

Excitement had me swirling in circles into the kitchen, dizzy with happiness. I'd made it. Today meant leaving for college, leaving home with no intention of returning. A new life for me. A life free from abuse. I didn't know what paths lay ahead, but I welcomed the change.

A car door slammed. My heart raced. It had to be Mom. I ran into my room, tripped over the braided throw rug beside the bed, and bumped against the nightstand. My gaze fell on a burn mark a cigarette etched on the cherry finish when Dad placed it there to free his hands. The wall beside it still showed where he'd slammed a fist, leaving a hole in the Sheetrock. A shiver ran down my spine. Plaster could never repair the damage done.

The side door opened. "Morgan, where are you?" my friend Janet called out.

I spun and headed for the family room, laughing, to greet her. We hugged briefly before I stepped back. "Hey, last night you didn't say anything about coming over. And why aren't you in school?"

"I wanted to surprise you, and give you this." Janet handed me a beautifully wrapped box. "Mom and I made it for you."

I perched on the couch and tore away the big white bow and pastel wrapping. After discarding the lid, I folded back white tissue paper and held up a stunning black sheath dress and matching jacket. "It's beautiful. Come help me try it on." I jumped up and led her down the hall to my room. The dress fit perfectly. Tears trickled down my cheeks as I ran my fingers over the detailed handiwork. "I love it."

She passed me a Kleenex. "No crying. Not today. This is a happy day for you. Let's get you packed."

I took off the dress and placed it in the largest of a three-piece luggage set Gram gave me for graduation. We then began some serious packing.

The phone rang. Janet clutched the blouse she'd been folding to her chest and remained quiet just in case. I swallowed hard and raced to answer before it rang a third time.

"I'll be home in fifteen minutes. Have everything ready to go."

I winced at Mom's agitated tone and turned away from Janet. "Yes, ma'am. I'm almost—"

She hung up.

My high school friends Becky and Mimi Clair were also attending Midway Mississippi Junior college. Two weeks ago, they invited me to ride with them in Mimi's new car—a graduation gift. Mom refused. She planned on taking me personally.

Janet and I said good-bye without ceremony. We knew my leaving didn't mean the end of our friendship. "Hey, I'll call you after I get settled and give you the dorm phone number." I waved as she drove away.

Five minutes later Mom's car sped into the driveway. Within minutes, she entered my bedroom, opened all three suitcases, and began going through everything. "You're not taking all these clothes." She removed the top layer of dresses and hung them in the closet. "It's not like you're leaving for good."

"But with my band scholarship, a lot of my weekends will be busy." I'd been chosen as one of five baton twirlers for the college band. But unlike high school, all Midway's games would be played on Thursday nights. A fact I hoped my mother didn't remember.

"Busy or not, you will come home, and you can get your clothing as you need it." She stormed out to dress for the trip.

For the past two years, I worked all winter at a local dollar store and all summer as a lifeguard. I paid for every one of the dresses. Determined more than ever not to return home, I placed each dress back in the luggage. Her footsteps marched toward me through the kitchen. With hands trembling, I snapped the cases shut and set them on the floor.

She swung the door wide. "Get this stuff loaded. This isn't a holiday for me."

When all my belongings were in the car, I waited for her in the den, fidgeting with the straps of my purse.

"Get in the car," Mom demanded as she headed for the carport door.

I followed her.

She hesitated. One hand gripped the doorknob, the other one rested by her side. My steps slowed until I stopped beside her. I'd seen that sly look too many times.

"Was Janet Barnes over here today?"

Before I could answer, she slapped me across the face. "Don't you lie, I can smell her perfume. You know how I feel about anyone being here while I'm at work." She raised her hand to slap me again. "Don't give me that look."

What look did I have other than fear? *Lord, please let her calm down.*

"You know, if it weren't for those two scholarships and the work program, you wouldn't be staying in the dorm, young lady. You'd be riding the bus home every day. One mess up and that's exactly where you'll find yourself. Do you understand me?"

My throat clogged. I struggled to hold back the tears. "Yes, ma'am."

Just a few more hours.

#

Once on campus, we found my dorm and checked in. The place swarmed with girls, their arms loaded with clothes, boxes, and electronics. Laughter, chatter, and blaring music coursed through the lobby, and no one seemed to mind.

"Why don't you go unpack while I locate your dorm mother." Mom scanned the vestibule. "She must be around here somewhere."

What was she up to?

"Go on," she demanded. "I'll be up later."

An attractive, well-dressed lady, my mom kept up with the latest fashions and styled her blonde hair in a popular French twist, like a model from *Vogue*. She wore a two-karat diamond ring on one hand and a slightly smaller one on the other.

In public, she cultivated her appearance of a good mom as carefully as she selected her clothes. I felt sure all the adults in our hometown thought of her as the perfect mother. Why would the dorm mother be any different?

Mom walked into my room as I hung up the last dress. I held my breath and hoped she wouldn't check the closet.

Her steel-blue eyes fixed on mine. There wouldn't be any good-byes. Ours wasn't an affectionate family. The words *I love you* came from my Gram. Hugs came from her also.

"I spoke with your dorm mother, and I'll stay in touch with her." She fired her parting shot. "Any problems and you'll find yourself back home." She didn't wait for a response. She didn't need one. Outside my door, her heels clicked on the tile floor. All other sounds diminished as her steps echoed in the hallway.

My whole body jolted when the stairway door slammed shut. With trembling legs, I dropped to the bed. Hugging my knees against my chest, I began rocking back and forth in a desperate attempt to calm myself. A steady stream of tears ran down my face, and pure fear ran through my body. Would I ever be free of their suffocating presence? Their punishments? The memories?

Their voices never stilled in the darkest depths of my mind. "You will tell us the truth! We know you had sex."

The images rolled unchecked—the two of them slapping my face.

Their promises still made my stomach clench. "Next time you'll end up in the county hospital."

My father's shouts, "Sit down. Stand up. When I get through with you, you'll ask how high."

The belt. "Put it in your dresser drawer so you don't forget."

And the stench of oil and metal. The gun barrel shoved in my face.

"God, please keep me safe."

Chapter 2

I sniffled and tried to force aside the fearful memories. "There." I placed the last of my personal items on the nightstand and stood back to admire my new home. The only splash of color was the Dutch-doll quilt from my great-aunt. The walls, floor, ceiling, and desk were stark white. Each end of the room mirrored the other. It wasn't much, but I liked it. This was my safe place for the next three months.

A knock interrupted my thoughts. "Morgan, are you in there?"

Becky's voice. I smiled and invited her in. "Hey, where's Mimi Clair?"

"Downstairs, waiting on us." Becky tugged on my arm. "Come on, get your purse."

"Where're we going?"

"Exploring. We're going to walk every square inch of this campus."

And, in spite of the heat, the three of us set out. My eyes wanted to take it all in. The vibrant red geraniums and pink petunias. The buildings constructed of red brick or cinder blocks. Cracks etched in the mortar. Ivy growing up the walls gave the campus a sense of charm. A smile stretched across my face. I stood tall and straight and took each step with ease. Somewhere deep inside me, hope stirred.

Mimi turned to face us as she walked backward. "Can you believe it? The three of us? Here? In college? We've entered a new stage in our life. No longer teenagers. We're adults now." She squinted then shielded her eyes from the sun. "Do you ever wonder where we'll be in four years? What we'll be doing?"

"I'm not sure." Becky slowed her pace and twirled a strand of her blonde hair with her finger. "Finishing college is part of my plan, for sure, but so is becoming the wife of a certain somebody we all know." Her big, blue eyes twinkled with a naughty glint. "The question is: which will come first?"

Mimi huffed aloud before turning to me. "How about you, Morgan? Where do you see yourself in four years?"

I'd learned not to allow my mind to wonder too far ahead or share my hopes and dreams with anyone—not even friends. "The only thing I can think about right now is my stomach. I'm starving. Why don't we find our way back to the cafeteria and have an early supper?"

We changed our course and hurried back the way we'd come. The wonderful smells of fresh yeast bread, cooked onions, and roast beef beckoned us. By the time we arrived, I was salivating like one of Pavlov's dogs.

"Look at all the people." Mimi craned around me in line. "I thought we'd be the first ones here."

"It's okay. Looks like the lines are moving fast enough. Besides, there's no place else to eat." My stomach rumbled.

"Sure there is." A girl in front of us turned around with a swish of her ponytail. "If you want a change and some really good food, Eddie's Restaurant is right across the street from the Administrations Office. They serve hamburgers the size of dinner plates. And their french fries come in a breadbasket. The foot-long chilidog's my favorite. Y'all should try it sometime."

"Hey thanks." Becky eyed the string of people ahead of us then faced me and Mimi Clair. "It sounds like a fun place. Maybe we should go."

"Now?" I gulped. I couldn't afford to eat anywhere other than the cafeteria. My parents made it clear. There'd be no help from them. All I had were the scholarships, the work program, and the money I'd saved.

Becky snickered. "Well you're the one 'starving.' I thought a good juicy hamburger—"

Shattering dishes interrupted. Laughter rang out. Near the front tables a tall, well-built guy bowed with one arm held in front of his waist, the other one in back, and food splattered all over his Levis. He then stood, laughing and waving at his audience while several cute girls and a worker picked up the scattered mess.

My face burned for him. He must be so embarrassed. I knew firsthand how to mask pain with humor.

"Who is that?" Mimi asked the girl with the ponytail.

"That bumbling klutz is our star linebacker. He plays a mean game, but graceful and smart he's not."

I cringed and remembered my own mother's words after I misspelled yet another word from the second grade speller. "She's too dumb. She'll never make *A*'s like her brother and sister," she stated as I mopped my own urine from the floor while Dad threaded his belt through his pant loops.

And I didn't. No matter how hard I tried or how severe the punishment.

"Here!" Mimi shoved her purse against my chest. "You girls hold my place in line while I see if the poor boy needs some more help."

#

When I returned to my room, a girl stood in the far corner hanging clothes in the other closet. She looked me over. "You must be my roommate. I'm Paige MacArthur."

"Hey, I'm Morgan."

Paige sauntered across the room with her head held high and her shoulders back. Not in a snobbish way, but very mature for her age. She stood at least five feet eight, a good six inches taller than me. She spoke in a quiet voice but not timid at all. "I got here later than planned. I guess what I don't finish unpacking can wait until after the meeting."

"What meeting?"

"The mandatory meeting with our dorm mother. Didn't you read the note? It was in your packet."

"I haven't looked at it yet."

"Don't worry. It doesn't start until seven, and I'll show you where to go." She reached for another hanger. "This is my second year at Midway. I know how overwhelming it can be at first, but you'll get used to things. And you'll love Mrs. Henderson."

"Who?"

"Mrs. Henderson—the dorm mother."

My stomach fluttered like I'd eaten a swarm of butterflies. I couldn't help but think about the conversation between my mother and the woman I was about to meet.

"Ready, Morgan?" Much too soon Paige asked.

The bedside clock showed six forty. "Do I have time to use the restroom?"

"Yes, but you need to hurry. We shouldn't be late."

By the time we arrived, all seats had been taken. Several girls sat on the floor, so we joined them.

An overweight, white-haired woman with deep dimples sat in a chair in front of the room, laughing and talking with some of the girls. At precisely seven o'clock, she stood, clapped her hands, and raised her voice. "Girls, may I have your attention? Quiet please. Our meeting tonight will be brief, I know many of you have put in a long day, and we all could use a good night's sleep. Let me start by introducing myself. My name is Mrs. Ruth Henderson. I've been at Midway Junior College for three years, and I'm proud to say, I'm the mother of two grown daughters. Being a parent brings me the greatest pleasure in life. My love for young ladies is the reason I continue to work in this capacity. Know my door is always open to you all."

She seemed nice enough. Still, I wondered about her sincerity. But it didn't matter. Through the years, I'd built a protective wall around myself, and not many people were allowed in.

"All doors," she continued, "will be locked and the alarms set at eight o'clock on Monday, Wednesday, and Sunday. Rooms will be checked at nine by girls designated as dorm monitors. All other nights, you must be in the dorm no later than ten and in your room by eleven. Anyone found out of their room after hours, will be written up. The first offense receives a warning. The second time you'll meet with me. If there's a third violation, the Dean of Women will become involved, along with your parents or guardians. Once the doors are locked, they will not be opened until six the following morning. Any girl leaving the campus at any time must sign out in this." She held up a wire-ringed, black notebook. "It is to be kept at the lobby desk at all times. You'll find a complete list of rules in the packet you received earlier today. Now, are there any questions?"

Several hands shot up. A pretty brunette asked, "Are we not allowed out of our rooms to use the bathroom?"

"Of course, but there will be no showering or brushing teeth after hours."

A tall girl in the back asked, "What if something unforeseen comes up? Can we call and let you know we're on our way?"

"Yes, by all means. But remember the rule. Anyone not in the dorm after the doors are locked will immediately be reported to the Dean of Women, who will notify your parents at once."

Girls began whining and complaining. One girl huffed, "Why don't they put us in prison and throw away the key?"

It was the sixties, and this college, located in the Deep South, took their responsibility for each of us seriously. To me, after all the oppression I'd suffered, this would be a cakewalk.

"Quiet girls, I know these rules may not meet with everyone's approval, but if you desire to live on campus, they must be followed. Now, I want you to know who your dorm monitors are."

When she called my name, I stood with the other five girls, smiled, and held my sweaty hands together, hoping no one could sense my apprehension. When she looked straight at me, my heart skipped a beat. What did my mother tell her? I shivered. Every move I made would be scrutinized, analyzed, and reported.

Well, at least I was forewarned. I'd be careful. There was one thing in my life neither she nor my parents could find out. Not yet.

Chapter 3

The next morning radios blared up and down the hall, belting out the sounds of The Beatles, Johnny Cash, Elvis, and some others I didn't recognize. The block walls may as well have been curtains, the noise penetrated with ease.

Paige threw back her bed linens. "So much for sleeping in."

"Will it be like this every morning?"

"I'm afraid so. A serene atmosphere and dorm life don't coexist."

"Well, at least we won't have to worry about being late for class." I yawned and punched the stem on my clock before the alarm went off.

With toiletries in hand, I made the short walk to the community bathroom where a fog of steam, perfume, hairspray, and other frou-frous sent me into a coughing fit. With so many girls, the room was close. Too close. And none of the lines seemed to be moving.

A tall blonde folded her arms across her chest and peered over the line. "If you're not cleaning your teeth, face, or hands, carry it back to your room gals."

A redhead stood at a lavatory with a head full of rollers. She turned and waved her toothbrush in the air. "Says who?"

"Look, I don't want to fight, but there are sixty-two girls on this floor. This is not the place to primp, pluck, or polish," the blonde firmly stated.

"You tell her, Pat," a voice cheered the blonde on.

Dorm monitor or not, at five two and 101 pounds, I'd let Pat, I believe they called the blonde, and the girl waving the toothbrush work this one out themselves. I edged away from Pat as they faced off. The next twenty seconds got pretty tense until, finally, the redhead rinsed her mouth, spit, picked up her belongings, and left.

By the time I made it back to the room, Paige walked out with towel and washcloth in hand.

"Good luck in there. I don't think all the rules have been clearly defined yet."

"Everybody'll get into the swing of things in a few days," she assured me before heading down the hall.

At last, a private moment. I scrambled into my clothes. Then I approached the mirror and attempted to brush my frizzy hair, which, in this muggy August air, surrounded my head rather than flowed from it like everyone else's. "Forget it." I tossed the hairbrush in the top drawer, convinced more than ever my grandfather was right.

"You've got cain't-cha don't-cha hair," he used to tease. "Can't you comb it and don't you try." Then he'd laugh.

But today was worse than ever. I secured the bushy heap with a headband. Still, I cringed over the image assessing me. Too many months of working at the city pool, exposed to sun and chlorine, bleached my long hair until it looked and felt like straw. Add to the mix, my lack of makeup, since Mom and Dad didn't allow it, and I felt like an odd duck around so many well-manicured girls.

I picked up books, paper, and pencil when someone called my

name from the hallway. "Morgan Selby, you're wanted on the phone."

Paige opened the door then leaned back toward the hall and shouted, "Yeah, she's still here."

I'd not given Janet the phone number yet, which only left one possibility. Rubbing my sweaty palms together, I took small strides toward the phone room.

My fingers gripped the dangling receiver. "Hello?"

"What do you mean taking all those dresses I rehung in your closet? You're such a conniving little wench. Well, you can bring them—every one—home this weekend, and we'll have a nice long talk. I think your father will help you understand and see things a lot clearer. Don't you?"

"I can't come home this weekend…I'm working."

"Doing what?"

"The dorm mother asked me to help with a special project. There are forms and other paperwork that needs completing."

"Well, we'll see about that. Maybe I'll give her a call. You better remember what I told you, young lady. Do you hear me?"

"Yes, ma'am," I spoke to dial tone.

I'd become a liar. I was fearful of my parents finding out and the consequences, but what about God? He knew.

I clasped the receiver with both hands. *I'm sorry. But I can't go home. You know what happens there.*

#

"Where were you this morning, Morgan?" Mimi folded her arms across her chest. "I thought we'd agreed to meet for breakfast. We went to your room and even looked for you in the bathroom. Becky and I barely had time to eat ourselves after spending so much time searching for you."

"I'm sorry, Mimi. Something came up."

"What, pray tell?"

"Mimi, you sound exactly like your mother," Becky scolded her roommate. "Don't pay her any attention, Morgan. Hey, we're headed over to Eddie's as soon as we dump our books. We can meet you back here in the lobby. Wanna come?"

"Maybe another time. I need to talk with Mrs. Henderson about something."

I stopped by the dorm mother's apartment and tapped lightly on the door. Life is sure strange. Twenty-four hours ago, I didn't want her to know my name. Now, I stood minutes away from entering her apartment and having a regular conversation.

"Yes?"

"Mrs. Henderson…uh…my name is Morgan Selby."

"Is there a problem?"

"No, ma'am. I wondered if we could talk?"

"Certainly." She held the door open wide. "Come in. What's on your mind?" She turned off the radio and gestured to the sofa. "Please, have a seat."

I took a slow, deep breath then forced a smile. "Mrs. Henderson, I wondered if you had some extra work for me. Not for pay or anything. You see, I'll be staying in the dorm most weekends, and extra work would help pass the time."

She glanced briefly at my hands clutched in my lap. "Well, thank you, Morgan. I didn't realize you lived so far away getting home would be difficult for you."

"It's a two-hour drive." What an idiot. Most of the girls lived that far or farther. No wonder one of her eyebrows shot up faster than I could shut my mouth.

"I can't think of anything, but let me give it some thought."

"Clean, file, anything?" I practically begged.

She uncrossed her legs and leaned forward. "Is there something else on your mind, Morgan?"

"No, ma'am." I hopped off the couch, more than ready to get out of there. "I'd better get going." I still needed to practice my twirling routine before supper.

#

The hot weather made it seem ridiculous to be wearing a coat over my shorts to and from the football field, but the college had clearly defined rules.

Right before I completed my routine for the second time, I heard a shrill whistle. I didn't look. Another whistle pierced the air, this time louder. I stopped and plucked my coat off the ground.

"Where you going in such a huff, Blue Eyes?"

"Chuck!" My heart leapt, and the worries of the day faded. I rushed toward him. "What are you doing here in the middle of a work week?"

"I decided to take the afternoon off and spend time with you." He leaned in for a kiss.

It had been so long since we'd dared to be seen together in public, to share a touch, a kiss, or an unhurried conversation. "How did you find me?"

He brushed a strand of hair out of my eyes. "You were walking to the football field when I drove into the parking lot."

"I didn't see you."

He smiled. "I know. What do you want to do tonight?"

"It's not a date night. I can't be out late."

"How about a steak supper?"

"I'd settle for a bologna sandwich," I teased. "As long as we can be together."

He winked. "Then it's a date. Can you be ready in forty-five minutes?"

"I think so, but don't come to the dorm. Mom spent a long time talking with the dorm mother. You know how my parents are. They'll do any and everything necessary to keep us apart. I wouldn't doubt if Mom gave her a picture of you."

Chuck pulled something from his pocket and cupped it in his hand, hiding it. "I have something of yours." His opened palm revealed a necklace with a small topaz stone. He'd given it to me the Christmas before my parents broke us up. They'd insisted I give it back.

"I can't believe you still have it." I caressed the dainty gold chain. "It's still beautiful. Would you help me put it on?" I held damp hair off my neck, while he fastened the clasp and then bent down and kissed me.

"How about we meet in front of the library?" He held my coat out for me to put on.

"I'll be there."

After a quick kiss, I headed toward the dorm. Giddiness washed over me. A real, honest-to-goodness, old-fashion date. It had been so long, I'd forgotten what it felt like. I had been cheated and robbed of life, but tonight, I wanted to feel alive.

Chapter 4

School was in full swing, and most afternoons I could be found on the field rehearsing for Thursday night's halftime. This week, the other four featurettes and I had been asked to do individual routines using fire batons.

After soaking each end in enough Kerosene to guarantee a long-lasting blazing flame, I stepped away from the fuel container and flicked the lighter. My fingers and hands controlled the swirling flame with ease. There was no fear. I'd been twirling fire since the eighth grade and never tired of its beauty. I tossed the baton high, turned two full circles, and grabbed it on its way down, never missing a beat. Then my ankle twisted. I stumbled forward. The odor of burning hair filled the air. I dropped the baton and slapped at my head with both hands. Adrenalin shot through my veins as I touched singed strands only half their original length.

Without a mirror, my imagination ran wild. Cringing, I scanned the bleachers. Empty. I released a breath. If only my coat would cover both my head and shorts. I snatched up the still-burning baton and placed it inside its case to extinguish the flame, then ran back toward the dorm, praying no one would see me. But the closer I got, people lined my path. Their snickers and chortles rose behind me.

When I finally reached my room and checked the mirror, I burst into tears, wrapped a towel around my head, and set out to find Jennifer. The one person who intrigued many of us with her flare for styling hair. The person whose room several of us gathered in nightly to laugh and talk about boys or the latest fashions. I listened a lot, but never added much. No one knew about Chuck, and of course, I had little to share when it came to style.

I found Jennifer in her room, reading. The door was ajar, so I tapped on the doorframe, walked in, and removed the towel.

She glanced up, her hand still holding her place on the page. A small smile slid onto her face then laughter consumed her. "What happened to you?"

"I guess the fire baton got too close…." No sense in trying to say another word. She laughed so hard, she fell back on the bed wheezing. I nudged the door closed before we had a full-blown audience, then plopped onto the edge of her bed and waited for her to regain her composure—fighting to contain mine. "If you could just come up for air long enough. Can you do anything with it or not?"

She started laughing again, her whole body shaking with spasms. Finally, she waved me away. "Go…go wash your hair. I'll be waiting."

When I returned, her room was full of the usual group. "What is this? Don't y'all have anything else to do?" I asked, unable to disguise the mortification in my voice.

Mimi sat on the window seat. Flakes of potato chips sprinkled on her chin and blouse. She shoved her hand into the bag. "Nope, we're here to watch Jennifer perform a miracle."

"You don't have an ounce of tact," Becky scolded Mimi before facing me. "We heard about what happened, Morgan, and not from Jennifer. We're all here to support you."

"Who told you?" I wanted to hide, crawl through a crack, evaporated into thin air.

"It doesn't matter." Jennifer pushed me in a chair.

I tried to cover my apprehension by telling myself it was only hair, but when the first long, wet hunk hit the floor, I lost it. "Wait a minute, Jennifer!"

I sprang to my feet and headed for the mirror, but she quickly plopped me back in the chair. "Honey, I've got to cut all the burned hair off. You've got to trust me. It'll look great when I'm done."

"Sorry, but I'm panicking." And why not, after today, everyone could call me Butch. "I don't know why. Whatever you do will beat what I've got now. It's not your fault there's not much to work with."

Within minutes, my hair lay scattered on the floor, and the girls responded with oooohs and aaaahs.

"Take a look." She handed me a mirror.

I didn't recognize myself. Never in a thousand years would I have picked such a modern do. She'd cut the right side above my ear and tapered it around the back, leaving the left longer, covering all but the lobe of that ear. She called it a "pixie".

"I love it." I couldn't stop staring.

"Told you, and we're not through."

Ann and Wendy stood with makeup bags in hand and removed colors of lipstick and base that "best matched my skin tone."

"Whoa, wait a minute. I'm not used to wearing—"

"Hang on." Wendy plucked cotton balls from a nearby bag. "When we're through, if you don't like it, you can wash it off."

An alcohol stench stung my nostrils as she began wiping my face. My eyes watered and burned. Once she finished, Ann applied a liquid base. This time they wanted me in front of the mirror as they explained every task. When they were through, the base covered my multiple freckles caused by the sun, the eye makeup made my blue eyes stand out. If someone didn't know me, they might not have noticed, but the slight change made a tremendous difference. For the first time in my life, I had facial qualities to marvel at, and I felt pretty. I couldn't believe it.

They then presented me with a small bag containing the very makeup they'd used.

"We'll help you until you get the hang of it." Jennifer patted my hair.

"I appreciate what you've done, but I can't take these things." I choked back tears.

Wendy stood behind me rubbing my shoulders. "It's our gift to you. Besides, those colors don't work for us anymore."

I looked around the room, making sure I caught every girl's eye. "Thank you."

Mimi clapped her hands and jumped to the floor. "Now that we have you all dolled up, can we go to supper? I'm starved."

"And don't forget." Jennifer grabbed Ann and spun around the room. "We're all going dancing tonight. Including you, Morgan."

"Oh, no. You've seen me try, so you know I can't dance. Besides, by the time we eat, find some place to kick up our heels...forget it. We wouldn't make it back on campus before Mrs. Henderson had all the doors locked."

"Wesley Hall." Jennifer let go of Ann. "I met some girls in my psychology class, and we've been invited to learn a new dance called the Tighten Up."

"Why can't we get together over here?" Mimi Clair asked. "Wesley Hall is the oldest girl's dorm on campus. It's awful."

"Because the girls who offered to teach us live in that old, awful dorm. They're black. I don't know if you noticed, Mimi, but almost all the black girls going to Midway live there."

"Why?" Becky asked. "Midway's been desegregated for a few years now."

"Jennifer and I've thought about it," Ann interjected. "We've concluded that the powers to be continue to segregate to the best of their ability. Why else would so many of them be staying in the same dorm?"

Wendy shook her head. "I don't think they could get away with doing that. There's got to be another reason."

"Maybe they're afraid."

Ann eyed me. "Afraid of what, Morgan?"

"Us, the unknown, the known. You forget Martin Luther King was killed, murdered a few months back. Not to mention the way some blacks have been treated in Mississippi. If you've never lived in fear, you wouldn't understand."

Mimi stood with her arms folded across her chest. "And what are you afraid of, Morgan?"

"I... Learning how to dance."

Everyone laughed.

#

After supper, most of us headed to the dimly lit building. Music vibrated the air even before we entered. I found a comfortable chair and sat, content to watch, but not for long.

A tall, thin black girl, who introduced herself as Shandra, pulled me to my feet. "You gone sit here all night, or you gone learn how to dance?"

"I don't...can't..."

"No? Well you gonna learn. I've seen you march in that band and twirl that baton. Anybody can learn." Shandra snapped her fingers to the beat and began to gyrate her hips. Elvis himself could've taken lessons. It didn't take long to realize how the dance got its name. If I attempted to duplicate her moves much longer, every muscle in my body would've been too tight by morning to get out of bed.

Shandra stopped dancing and threw up her hands. "It must be true what they say about some white people not having a lick of rhythm, 'cause you one of 'em."

But her teasing didn't stop me from trying.

The hour passed much too quickly. Jennifer invited them to visit us the following night. Sadly, they didn't.

#

By three forty-five on Friday afternoon, many of the girls, including Paige, had already left for the weekend. The dorm was quiet. I'd just returned to my room from a shower and had removed my robe when Becky walked in. I grabbed a towel and quickly turned to cover myself, but it was too late.

Becky gasped. "Morgan, your back. What happened to your back?"

I shoved my arms through the robe sleeves and fumbled with the sash before tying it tightly. I couldn't make myself look at her. "Are you packed and ready to leave?"

She flopped down in the chair next to the desk and slung her purse in the floor. "I'm not going anywhere until you tell me what happened to your back."

My head throbbed, keeping pace with my heart. I looked out the window, determined not to respond.

"Who did that to you, Morgan? We've been friends for years, and you've never said a word."

"Becky, I can't—" My throat closed.

"Why? Are you afraid I'll tell? Are you afraid I might...Your parents did this, didn't they?"

I hesitated then nodded.

Silence filled the room. Then I heard Becky's footsteps and felt the warmth of her hand on my shoulder. "We've got to get you some help. My father could contact a lawyer—"

"No!"

"Why not?"

I faced her. "I've already talked with a lawyer. A year ago, someone made me an appointment and paid the bill. I never knew who. The lawyer told me he couldn't do anything without proof of abuse. I told him I was wearing it. Long story short, he told me it would be almost impossible to be taken from my parents, and advised I wait until my eighteenth birthday."

"Then Dad will find another lawyer."

"No. I appreciate what you're trying to do, but I'll be eighteen in three months."

"So what!"

"The State of Mississippi will acknowledge me as an adult then. My parents will no longer have legal authority over me. Until then, I intend to stay right here."

Becky's lip quivered. "Is there *anything* I can do?"

"Keep my secret."

"I won't tell."

"Not even your parents?"

"Not a soul." She held her hand up as if taking a solemn oath. "Promise. But I'm curious...I know your mother and father made you stop seeing Chuck, but did he ever know about the abuse?"

Should I tell her everything? "Chuck and I never stopped seeing one another. It wasn't easy. But there were opportunities after basketball games, band practice, before or after work. We've seen each other every weekend since I've been at Midway."

Becky wiped trails of mascara from her cheeks. "Does he know about your back?"

"He's never seen it, and to tell him about the marks would only create further anguish. But I've talked to him about my parents and the problems at home, hoping he could help me understand." Those last words clogged my throat. I dug my fingernails into each palm and tried to contain the anger wanting to bust free. "My parents profess to be Christians. Dad's been a deacon for years." I looked Becky in the eye. "Can you tell me how parents, who are supposed to love and protect their children, do such cruel things?"

She broke eye contact. "I don't know."

I sat on the edge of the bed. "Me, either."

"Have your parents always been…I don't know what word to use—hateful?"

"As far back as I can remember."

"What about Marsha and Wayne?"

"My parents didn't play favorites, if that's what you're asking. The three of us just always knew if Mom became agitated, bad things happened. And Dad *always* got involved."

"Why did you keep it hidden all this time?"

"Fear's a powerful weapon, Becky."

"And you never stood up to 'em?"

"Nope. I've never been strong enough. Marsha did, and it paid off for her. But I don't have it in me, and they know it. And I don't know how much more I can take."

Chapter 5

After Becky left, I stretched out on the bed and rested my eyes. When I woke, the afternoon shadows had advanced far into the room.

"It can't be!" I blinked at the bedside clock then jumped out of bed. In forty minutes, Chuck would be in front of the library waiting. A quick glance in the mirror caused another wave of panic to wash over me. Strands of short hair stuck straight up. My new do a total mess.

I grabbed my brush, hairspray, hairdryer, and the makeup the girls had given me and dashed through the hall to the bathroom. Taking a deep breath, I wet my hair in the sink and got to work styling it the way Jennifer had shown me. A little spritz of hairspray held it in place. I could imagine the minutes ticking away as I cleaned off smudged makeup and smoothed on a little foundation, added blush and mascara, then lipstick…there. Chuck was in for a surprise.

Back in my room, I plundered my closet and chose a dark blue, A-line dress with a matching jacket and added the topaz necklace Chuck had given me. One last look in the mirror—perfect—and with little time to spare.

Before I reached the front of the library, I saw Chuck standing by his gray Mustang with one of his long legs propped on the front tire. His silky, light-brown hair and brown suit complemented his ruddy complexion. He studied the sky, unaware of my approach.

"Didn't your mother teach you any manners?" I teased.

"Morgan?" He walked to where I stood. "What happened to your hair?" He reached up and moved my head from side to side, studying Jennifer's handiwork.

"Do you like it?" Please don't lie to protect my feelings.

"Turn around. Let me see the back."

"Tell me the truth. You don't like it, do you?"

He spun me around, leaned in, and kissed me on the lips then on the neck. "Yep, I like it a lot. Kissed you and didn't get one single hair in my mouth."

"Oh, you." I sputtered and stepped away.

He moved closer, grabbed my waist, and held me against his body. "Let's try that again."

Our nearness caused my heart to race. I'd never known a love like this before. How easy it would be to go beyond the boundaries Christ clearly set. To do the very thing my parents accused me of.

But I could still hear my mamaw's words from my younger years. "Let your privates be your privates." Strange, simple words, but I knew what she meant. And with time, her words became clearer, even though she'd been gone for two years now.

I pulled away. "We'd better get going."

Chuck sighed then kissed my nose. "You're right. We've got a lot to do. I have the night all planned. We're having dinner at Michael's, but you get to choose the movie."

We drove to Michael's and found the parking lot packed.

"We can go somewhere else if you want to." The meal would probably be way too expensive anyway.

He glanced at me sideways and winked. "Remember you pick the movie, and I pick the restaurant."

He really did have the night planned. To my amazement, Chuck had made reservations, and the hostess seated us almost immediately.

After ordering, Chuck reached for my hand. "You're beautiful. I don't think I've ever seen you wear lipstick."

"It's the girls at the dorm. We've become such good friends. They've taken me under their wings."

"So the girls talked you into the new hairstyle?"

"Well, that's a long story." I squeezed lemon into my iced tea.

"I love long stories," he said with that cute, flirtatious grin of his.

"All right. I'll tell you, but you have to *promise* not to laugh."

"I promise. Scout's honor." He tapped two fingers to the side of his forehead.

I peered straight into his baby blues. "You were never a scout."

"My parents couldn't afford the uniform, but I would've been otherwise. I had the book."

"Okay, but if you laugh..." Giving him a final warning look, I continued, "I singed my hair while twirling the fire baton."

"Before or during halftime?" His voice cracked. "I mean, did they come out with a fire extinguisher, or did you have to drop and roll?"

The couple next to us gawked as Chuck laughed.

I picked up the cloth napkin and buried my face.

"I'm sorry, Morgan. Please don't cry." He reached over and rubbed my arm. "I'm stupid and insensitive. Honey, please don't cry."

I couldn't continue the charade any longer. I removed the napkin and continued to laugh. "Got you back."

"I love you, Morgan Selby." He pressed my hand to his lips.

The waitress interrupted the special moment by delivering our meal. After blessing the food, we took our time eating and enjoyed each other's company. We lost track of the hour.

Chuck glanced at his watch. "We won't make it to the movies tonight."

"That's all right. Like my great-uncle Laverne used to say, 'It don't get no better than this.'"

"It will someday."

"What do you mean?"

"I won't always be taking you back to the dorm and saying good night."

Maybe *someday.*

#

Chuck drove me back to the campus. As we neared the dorm, Mrs. Henderson was standing at the front door. I slid down in the seat, hoping she hadn't seen me. "Don't stop."

"I see her." He made a slow U-turn and headed for the library parking lot. "I'll walk you as far as I can. Maybe she won't be out there."

But she was. As we got closer, she reminded me of a mamma dog waiting for one of her stray pups to return. I hoped the stray wasn't me.

"I've got to go, Chuck." I let go of his hand. "I'm a nervous wreck."

"Don't be."

"What if Mom's called? Where do I say I've been?"

"Out with a friend. I'll stand here until you get inside. Glance at the sky if everything's okay. Otherwise, I'll go get the car and come after you. I won't let your parents hurt you again, Morgan."

He held me tight and kissed me. "It's okay. I'll pick you up Sunday for church. Remember the signal." He pointed up.

I approached the dorm steps and plastered a smile on my face. "Hi, Mrs. Henderson."

"You're very dressed up tonight. I haven't checked the sign out sheet, but nothing on campus would constitute such attire. I trust you didn't leave the grounds. As a monitor and a student, it would result in unfavorable consequence for you."

"Yes, ma'am. But with it being such a glorious night, seems neither of us could stay cooped up in our rooms. Just look at 'em. The moon. The stars." Who could wish for a more perfect evening?

Chapter 6

Becky ran into my room and slammed the door. "Morgan! Your mother's downstairs talking with the dorm mother."

Almost a week had passed since Chuck took me to Michaels and Mrs. Henderson questioned me about leaving the campus without signing out.

I studied Becky's pale face. I'd never seen anyone's eyes so wide. She held a hand to her chest and struggled to catch her breath. This wasn't a prank.

"Why! Why can't she leave me alone?" I tried not to panic. If Mrs. Henderson had called her, if Mom had suspected anything, she would've been here long before now.

My hands began to shake, my teeth chatter. I'd not heard from Mom but once since school started, and I was beginning to think out of sight, out of mind. Now, without warning, she showed up a few hours before the Thursday night football game. I struggled to get enough air into my lungs. "Is Dad with her?"

"I don't think so. Do you want me to go check?"

"No. Help me get into this uniform. If anyone asks, you haven't seen me."

Becky zipped the back of my red sequin outfit. "What are you going to do?"

"I've got to get out of here. I don't know what she's up to, but it can't be good. One of my biggest fears has been that my parents would remove me from Midway and force me back home."

Her voice lowered to a whisper. "Do you think she knows about Chuck?"

"I don't think so. She may have her suspicions, but if she had any proof, I'd already know about it. Believe me; my parents wouldn't hesitate to 'teach me a lesson.'"

"Maybe your mother is here to watch you perform at halftime. Or to take you out to eat."

"No way. I don't expect you to understand." I slipped my majorette boots on and picked up my baton and coat. "If I'm forced to go home with her tonight, will you let Chuck know?"

Becky nodded. "Sure, I'll phone him."

To avoid contact with Mom, I hurried to the far end of the hallway and crept down the stairs. I used the side door to leave the building and practically ran until I reached my destination. No one would think to look for me in the auditorium.

I hid behind the stage curtain and paced. What if she does make me go back home with her? What am I going to do? How will I ever get away again? What if she *has* found out about Chuck? *Oh, God, please...please!*

At six thirty, after more than an hour, I left my place of hiding and walked to the band hall. With every step, I scanned the area for Mom. My heart raced, matching the rapid drumbeat. At six fifty, the band moved to our section of the bleachers. Right after we sat in unison, someone grabbed my foot. An uncontrollable scream burst from my mouth.

The band director peered over his glasses at me. "What seems to be the problem, Morgan?"

"Nothing. I'm fine. Sorry."

He smiled and shook his head before refocusing on his music folder.

I leaned over and peeked through the stands. "You scared the devil out of me, Becky."

"Sorry, but I thought you'd like to know about your mother."

"Did she or the dorm mother ask you anything?"

"No. I never saw your mother again. But Ann said she sat in your room for twenty minutes before she came to her room and asked about you. By the way, she's perched herself halfway down, three rows from the top."

"Okay. Thanks, Becky."

I tried to think of what to do. I knew the night wouldn't end without a conversation of some type, so I decided to get it over with.

I stood and scanned the area Becky described and spotted Mom. Then I walked to the director's podium and waited for him to complete his conversation with a faculty member.

"Did you have a question, Morgan?"

"No, sir. I have a request. My Mom has driven more than two hours to get here, and I've not seen her yet. I wondered if you'd allow me to…?"

"Fine, go, but make your visit brief." Again, he looked over the frame of his glasses. "No longer than fifteen minutes."

It took a little time to weave through the crowded bleachers. I felt like a mouse that didn't have any better sense than to walk up to a hungry snake. But Mom didn't seem to notice my approach. I sat beside her. She never flinched.

I was short of breath, more from raveled nerves than the climb. "Why did you sit way up here?"

"So I could see what I needed to." She kept her eyes focused on the ball field.

"I didn't know you were here." Another lie. "Is there something wrong?"

"No." She turned and glared at me. "What have you done to your hair?"

"One of the girls in the dorm cut it for me. Do you like it?"

"No, I don't." She scanned me from my head to my boots then shook her head. "You should've had a professional cut it, rather than wasting your money on makeup that makes you look like a clown—or worse."

Her words cut like a knife. I ached to tell her I didn't think there would be enough money to purchase the personal toiletries needed to get me through the month, much less enough money for an appointment at a salon. But knowing how she'd respond, I kept my mouth shut. As usual.

"Where were you earlier?" She narrowed her eyes and stared straight into mine. "I sat in your room for forty-five minutes waiting for you."

"I'm sorry, Mom. I needed to practice my routine for tonight, and the auditorium seemed like the logical place to go. If you had called to let me know you were coming—"

"I don't need to call you, and you'll *never* know when I'll show up next." She raised her voice for all to hear.

Hurt, embarrassed, and on the verge of tears, I lowered my head and spoke in a hushed tone, "The band director told me not to be gone long. I have to play the clarinet while we're in the stands. Maybe I'll see you after the halftime show."

But she didn't stay for halftime, she walked right past where I sat and never glanced up.

I squeezed my eyes shut, placed a hand to my chest, and rocked ever so slightly in an attempt to calm myself. I'd made it one more night.

#

After the game, I returned to the dorm and changed out of my uniform and into a comfortable dress. One of our jobs as dorm monitors was to man the lobby desk during certain hours. Since Chuck never came up during weekday nights, and most everyone else had dates, I volunteered to work every Thursday after the game.

I'd been at the desk less than five minutes when Mrs. Henderson approached.

"Who won the game?"

"We did, seven to zero."

We looked at each other in silence for a brief moment. "Your mother wanted to surprise you today with a visit, did she find you?"

"Yes, we spoke." I'd learned the hard way, the less said, the safer.

"You know I could've gotten someone else to work the desk tonight. Y'all could've gone out to eat and spent some time together."

I jerked my head toward her. "Mrs. Henderson, my mom didn't even stay for halftime."

Another moment of silence. "Well, I'll let you get back to your work. Good night, Morgan."

She walked back to her apartment. Guilt ate away at me for being so short with her.

I tapped my short-clipped nails against the desk. Why had Mom come? Did she expect to find Chuck at the ballgame? We weren't that careless. Why couldn't Mom accept that she would someday lose control over me? Did she savor the sight of fear and pain in my eyes and celebrate her ability to produce it? The same old question. No new answers.

#

Chuck and I met Friday evening at the time and place we'd grown accustomed to. Even after Mrs. Henderson's admonishment, I still didn't sign out in the required ledger. It was a risk I had to take. If Mom called, she'd question the dorm mother demanding to know with whom, where, and when I'd be back. Unless someone witnessed my departure or did a room search, everyone would assume I remained in the dorm.

"I've missed you." Chuck leaned in for a kiss. "I thought we'd go to a movie tonight, but the only one rated G is *Planet of the Apes.*"

"Fine." I gave him a halfhearted smile.

"You want to see *Planet of the Apes*?"

"What? No. Unless you do."

"Okay, what's wrong? I know last night when I called, you were upset about your mother showing up. Is it still bothering you?"

"*Yes.* Why wouldn't it? What if she'd decided to show up tonight or Sunday? We'd be caught off guard. There'd be no way for me to get in touch with you, and God help us both if they were to ever catch us together."

Chuck reached for my hands and held them close to his chest. "Morgan, I love you. You've been through a lot. But your parents have to realize they can't hold you captive forever. They've got to face the facts: you're not a child anymore."

"Oh, yeah? Well, you explain to me why she drove all the way up here yesterday?" I pulled my hands away and crossed my arms. "I'll tell you why. She thought you'd be here. When you weren't, she couldn't resist the chance to tell me how ridiculous I looked wearing makeup. She suggested next time I should pay someone to style my hair. What does she think I'd use for money? I can't buy deodorant, much less pay for anything extra."

Chuck didn't respond. He just sat there staring at me.

"What?" I searched his eyes for something I'd missed.

"How many times have I asked if you needed money? I even offered, but you refused. You've told me multiple times not to worry. Now I find out you can't buy personal necessities! That…that you don't have any money."

"I never said I didn't have any money."

"How much do you have?"

"That's none of your business. We're not married." Heat rushed to my neck and face.

"Morgan Selby, you have a pride issue you need to check."

"Don't you dare—"

"Yes, I will. You know as well as I do what God has to say about a prideful heart."

"'Pride goeth before destruction.' What's your point?"

"Pride in a small dose can be a good thing. Too much, and you'll end up as bitter, angry, and hurtful as your parents."

"I've got to make it on my own or do without. It has nothing to do with pride."

"Then what would you call it?"

I took a deep breath. "How do I make you understand?"

"Talk to me. Tell me why you don't trust me enough to let me help you."

"It has nothing to do with trust." I faced him. "One night, our parents allowed my brother and sister and me to go to a carnival. Anyway, they gave us all the same amount of money. I spent all mine, but a friend wanted me to do a cakewalk with her. Long story short, she purchased two tickets and gave me one. When Dad arrived, it hadn't ended yet. On the way home, he questioned me about it. I told him. He got mad. After I was punished, he said, 'If you don't have, you do without.' I never forgot the lesson."

"Morgan, I can't have money in my pocket and watch you go without. We've talked about marriage, but without trust it'll never work."

He took his billfold out of his pocket and placed it in my hands. His gaze moved from one of my eyes to the other, as if searching for an answer.

Chapter 7

The door to my room sailed inward without anyone bothering to knock. "You're going to freak out, Morgan."

"What did you say, Mimi?" I crawled from under my desk with the dropped pencil in hand and came face-to-face with a luxurious bouquet of a dozen, long-stem red roses. Their fruity aroma surrounded me.

Mimi beamed. "I happened to be in the lobby when the florist made the delivery."

I stood and straightened my skirt. "They're beautiful. You must be so excited. Who sent them?"

She rolled her eyes. "You ditz, these are for you."

I tossed the pencil. "For me? Are you sure?"

"Uh-huh." She plucked a small envelope from the middle of the flowers and handed it to me. "Your name's on the outside, but I'm more interested in the name on the inside."

I'd never received roses before. They had to be from Chuck. Now it would be impossible to keep our relationship hidden from the girls in the dorm…or from my parents. I'd never known Mimi to be discreet.

I opened the envelope, read the note, and breathed a sigh.

"Well?"

I waved the card in the air and sang, "I've got a secret admirer."

"Let me see that." Mimi snatched the card, glanced at it, then at me with her eyebrows bunched together. "Who do you think it is?"

I shrugged and leaned down to smell the bouquet's sweet fragrance. "There's not a name on the card, but the vision in my mind has him tall and handsome."

"Wait till the girls hear about this. They'll flip." She opened the door and flounced out.

The rest of the afternoon, I received an onslaught of inquiries about my mystery fellow. The list of suspects grew. Of course, Becky knew, but she went along with the game.

Chuck called later to confirm our date for Friday.

"Thanks for the roses. They're beautiful." I hadn't stopped smiling since they arrived. "The girls have been making some pretty wild speculations about who sent them. It's been a fun day."

"I'm glad you're enjoying them. I've got more surprises planned for this weekend."

"What?"

"If I told you, then it wouldn't be a surprise." He toyed with me. "Don't ask any more questions. I'll see you Friday night."

"Wait. You have to give me a hint."

"I love you, Morgan." His soft, sexy voice sent chills through my body.

I felt like a child on Christmas Eve. What did he have planned?

#

Curiosity and anticipation made it difficult to focus in any of my classes.

By four o'clock Friday afternoon, less than a dozen of us

remained in the dorm. The rest of the girls had packed their suitcases with haste, ready to leave for the weekend. I wondered, but never asked any of those who stayed behind why they didn't go home. And hoped they never asked me either. I found comfort in the quietness and really didn't mind being by myself.

I took a long shower and chose a special dress for the night. As I tried to decide what shoes to wear, someone knocked at the door.

"Come in."

The door opened, and Mrs. Henderson walked in.

I jolted. We'd conversed on several occasions, but for her to come to my room, to seek me out....I swallowed. This didn't feel right.

"Hi, Morgan, how are you this evening?"

"I'm fine, thank you." But I wasn't fine. I felt sick to my stomach.

She waved her hand toward a chair. "May I sit down?"

"Sure." My mouth felt so dry I could hardly speak. I perched on the edge of the bed and placed both of my hands under my thighs to hide their trembling.

"I know you've not been home since school started, and I wondered if you needed to talk."

"No..." Did my smile look as fake as it felt? "I don't think so."

She eyed me, as if waiting for me to change my mind.

Forcing myself to breathe normal, I held her gaze. And my tongue.

After several excruciating seconds, she spoke. "I received a call from your mother today. She wanted to know why you had to work every weekend and how much longer I'd need your help."

A blast of adrenalin sped my heart rate. "What did you tell her?"

"I told her you were working on a project for me and hopefully it would be finished soon." She leaned forward. "Why don't you tell me what's going on?"

Tears stung my eyes, and my chin began to quiver. "Mrs. Henderson, I can't go home."

"Are you in trouble?"

"What do you mean?"

"Morgan, I've been a dorm mother for the past three years. There have been a few girls along the way who made mistakes and got themselves in predicaments. The kind that can only be hidden for so long."

It took me a minute to realize what she'd accused me of. I jumped up from the bed and held my robe against my flat stomach. "I'm not pregnant. You can't get pregnant if you've never had sex."

"I'm sorry. I wasn't trying to imply—"

"Yes, you were." I glared at her with my jaw clenched.

She covered her mouth with her hand and stared at the floor. The room was quiet.

"You're right, and I'm sorry." She leaned back in the chair and studied me. "Please accept my apology."

I was so mad I couldn't speak. Finally, I nodded.

"Can I ask why you don't go home? It's not because of the distance. Your friends, Mimi and Becky, are from Greer, and they go home every week."

I fought a mental battle, torn between telling the whole ugly truth and keeping my mouth shut. I straddled the fence.

"When my mother calls, I tell her I'm working, because I never want to go back there again. There's nothing else to tell."

I squirmed as the room became quiet for only seconds before she continued. "All right. I won't pry further. I know there's a problem, and it's okay if you don't want to talk about it now. But know I'm here if you ever need anything."

She stood and walked toward the door.

Panic overrode my anger. "If my mother calls again, what will you tell her?"

She took a step toward me. "I don't know. I'm not in the habit of lying. In fact, I've never lied for a student before today. I just wish you'd trust me." Before she left the room, she glanced at the roses then back at me. "He's got good taste."

She knows. Maybe not every detail, but enough to get me pulled out of here. According to the calendar on the wall, there were six more weeks until my birthday.

I knew Chuck had to be in the parking lot by now. I finished dressing, checked my reflection, and practiced a smile. Whatever he had planned for tonight, my emotional state was not going to mess things up.

I left the dorm using the side door as usual. When I walked outside, Chuck stood there waiting.

"Hey." He reached for my hand. "I left my car at the library. If we walk along the back toward the football field, your dorm mother won't be able to see us."

"Let's go." I gave him a smile like the one I practiced in my room.

"What's wrong?"

"Nothing." I kept the smile plastered in place.

"You're not a good liar...with or without the smile."

"It's not a big deal. I'm really okay."

"I know you, Morgan. You're upset. I see it in your eyes."

"You're right, but let's walk and talk at the same time."

We began the roundabout path back to his car while I explained about Mom's phone call to Mrs. Henderson, which led to her conversation with me.

"It sounds like she cares and has figured out there's a problem between you and your parents. Maybe you should level with her."

I shook my head. "No way. I can't take a chance."

"What if she wants to help?"

I stopped and faced him. "*No.*"

"Okay. You know her. I don't."

Chuck's arm was around me as we walked to the passenger side of the car. He pulled me to him. Feeling safe and loved, I relaxed in his arms and no longer worried about the what-ifs.

#

We drove a short distance to the restaurant Chuck had chosen. Outside it had the look of an old colonial home. The inside was grand. The antique chandeliers hanging from the high ceilings and the rustic fireplace gave it a romantic touch. The hardwood floors, linen-covered tables, and the silver pieces added to the charm.

Chuck requested a table close to the fireplace and told the hostess he'd let her know when we were ready to order. "We'd like some time alone."

"Wow. When you plan a surprise, you go all out."

"I want you to remember this night when we're old and gray."

"Why? What are you up to?"

He took my hand and rubbed the back of it with his thumb. "Because the night someone asks you to marry him should be special and always remembered."

"Are you…*did* you… ask me to marry you?" My stomach fluttered.

A broad smile spread across his face, and an extra twinkle lit his eyes. "Why do you act so surprised? I love you. We've talked about marriage several times. Tonight I want to make it official. Morgan Selby, will you marry me?"

I sucked in a breath as tears ran down my face. “Yes!”

Chuck bounced out of his chair and moved to my side of the table. He cradled my face in his hands and kissed both cheeks before pressing his lips gently against mine. And it didn’t matter that others might be watching.

He rested his forehead on mine. “I want us to get married as soon as possible.”

I pulled back. “I’m not even eighteen. There’s no way we can legally get married without my parents’ signature, and we both know that’ll never happen.”

“What if there is a way?”

“How?”

He cupped my hands with his. “In the State of Alabama, you can marry when you’re eighteen.”

“You can? How do you know?”

“My older sister works at the courthouse in Yalobusha County. She did the research and gave me the details.”

“And it would be legal? Even the State of Mississippi would see us as married?”

He smiled and nodded. “What do you say?”

Chapter 8

The following Sunday, Chuck and I walked down the church aisle hand in hand. He leaned in and asked in a soft voice, "Do you think you'll look back someday and have regrets?"

The pastor greeted us before I had a chance to answer, then we chose a pew and sat.

People next to us smiled and welcomed us. When things began to quiet down, I nudged him. "Regrets about what?"

"Not having a big church wedding."

I shook my head. "No. Marsha had a well-planned ceremony with all the trimmings: friends, family, beautiful dress, catered reception. What a disaster. The problem was, the plans were all Mom's, from the choice of bridesmaids, to the music. By the time Marsha and Bob took their vows, I didn't think either one of them were happy."

He placed an arm around my shoulders and gave me a squeeze as the service began.

Later, over lunch, Chuck convinced me we could work out all the details and marry two days after my birthday. I needed a copy of my birth certificate. The original was in a metal box in Mom's closet. I had no intentions of retrieving it.

Chuck took a pen from his shirt pocket and wrote on a clean napkin. "I'll check in Jackson about a form for a replacement, see how long it'll take to get here, and call you tomorrow night."

I brushed a fingernail across my lower lip and stared out the restaurant window.

"What's wrong, Morgan?"

"We've got to be careful with every detail and make sure my parents don't get wind of our plans. They'll do everything in their power to stop us, and don't *ever* forget about Dad's threat."

Chuck gathered my hands in his. "Your father doesn't want to spend the rest of his life in prison. He's not going to kill me. He said it to scare you."

"He put the gun in my face and swore to God he'd kill you before ever allowing us to be together." The vision of that night replayed in my mind, and as if someone placed their hands around my throat, I couldn't breathe.

"Come on. Let's get out of here."

Once in the car, Chuck cradled my face with his hands and pressed his forehead against mine. "Morgan, do you trust me?"

"You know I do."

"Then listen to me. Your parents are never going to hurt you again. They've done and said horrible things to you, but it's time to take that power away from them. Once we're married, whether they accept it or not, there's nothing they can do about it, or to you. I won't allow it. You've got a decision to make. Do you want to continue to give them the freedom to hurt you, or will you take a stand and say enough is enough? It won't happen overnight, but with time, it will."

Tears filled my eyes. "I know what you're saying, but I'm afraid. You don't know what it's like. After so many years, how can I change? How do you face someone who's been so cruel and say,

'I'm not afraid of you anymore?'"

He removed his hands from my face, reached into his pocket for a handkerchief, and handed it to me. "You take it one step at a time. We'll walk this road together." He gently eased my head to his shoulder.

I'd cried so much over the pain my parents had caused. Now my tears fell as the truth sank in. I had someone on this earth who knew, understood, and loved me enough to stand, not beside me, but in front of me, to protect me. Finally, I began to acknowledge that the dark days and physical pain were coming to an end. For the first time in my life, I felt a sense of relief. God had answered my prayers.

When there were no more tears left, I raised my head from Chuck's shoulder and drew in a deep breath. Black marks from my mascara smeared his handkerchief and shirt. I adjusted the rearview mirror, dabbed at my raccoonish smudged eyes, and then turned to him pointing at my face. "How can you love this?"

He touched me above my left breast with his finger. "I know your heart. I love who *you* are."

I'd never experienced true, unconditional love from another human. Other than my salvation, Chuck was the greatest gift God had ever given me.

He smiled and ran the back of his hand down my cheek. "What day this week do you want to make a trip to Alabama? We'll see a lawyer and find out all the legalities about getting married. I think it'll help us both."

We decided to make the trip Friday morning. I'd have to skip all my classes, but I needed to know my parents wouldn't legally be able to erase the vows we'd be making to God and each other.

#

That evening, after Chuck left and the girls returned from their visits with parents and friends, the usual group met in Jennifer's room to discuss our weekend adventures.

Mimi sat on the edge of the desk with her feet propped on the garbage can. "What'd you do this weekend, Morgan? You act like you've had a dose of nitrous oxide. I don't think I've ever seen you so happy. Did you hear from your secret admirer?"

"You wouldn't believe me if I told you."

"That means you did hear from him." The wastebasket slipped from under her feet and rolled across the floor. She sprang from the desk, picked up the spilled items, and continued with her questions. "Did y'all go out? What's his name? What does he look like?"

"Good grief, Mimi, you'd think you were her mother instead of a friend," Wendy scolded. "Leave her alone."

I leaned over and whispered as if she were the only one privy to my secret. "No, I don't mind telling you. He did call, and we went out Friday night. He's very nice looking, tall, well-mannered, madly in love, and wants to marry me."

Mimi curled up her lip and banged the metal can back in its place. "Right."

The room burst into laughter. Mimi crossed her arms and scowled at us. The focus changed when Ann broke in talking about the latest love of her life. After another hour, and two large bags of potato chips, we each left, headed for our own rooms.

Later, Becky sauntered into my room and sat beside me on the bed. "What are you up to?"

I closed my notebook. "Homework, and I'm ready for a break."

She took off her shoes and pushed herself farther on the bed. "I thought I'd visit you and find out what really happened this weekend."

"Oh, you know the same old thing: washed my clothes, cleaned the room, watched television, slept, did homework, went to church."

"Bless your heart. Well, you better not keep hanging onto that same old story. Some of the girls are ready to play cupid. Especially if your 'secret admirer' doesn't hurry up and materialize."

"Oh, please. Can't you hold them off a little longer?"

"I'll try, but sooner or later, you'll have to produce Chuck or come up with some mighty big reason why you don't date."

"All I need is six more weeks."

"Why six weeks?"

"I turn eighteen, remember? Besides," I scrambled off the bed, closed the door, and reclaimed my spot next to her, "Chuck and I'll be married by then, and I want you to be my maid of honor."

Her mouth dropped open, but the room remained quiet for a split second before she squealed and shook me by the shoulders. Then she gave me a serious looking over. "Do your parents know?"

"No, and they can't find out." I couldn't hold it in another second. I told her everything, including our plans to elope.

"Girl, I wouldn't want to be in the same town with your parents when they find out. Aren't you scared?"

"Of course I'm scared. That's why we've planned a trip to Alabama this Friday to talk with a lawyer."

Becky took her maid of honor role seriously and wanted to skip classes and go with us to Alabama. Chuck liked the idea and invited his best friend and best man, Kyle, along.

#

At seven Friday morning, Becky and I walked to the library parking lot, where Chuck and Kyle were waiting. After stopping for breakfast, we began the four-hour trip to Vernon, Alabama.

Once we arrived, Chuck scanned the lawyers in the yellow pages. The third one listed, Patricia Bennett, said she could see him if he came in a half hour. By the time we found her office, we had less than fifteen minutes to wait in the parking lot. The food I'd eaten earlier now fought with my jittery stomach.

Kyle's arm rested across the back of the front seat as he twisted to face Chuck. "Becky and I'll wait out here while you two take care of business."

"Are you ready?" Chuck opened his door and held it while I slid across the seat and stepped out. He laced his fingers with mine and smiled. "I love you, Morgan."

His words chased away my uneasiness and bathed me with warm contentment. "I love you, too."

"Then let's go get some answers." He led me down the pebbled sidewalk to the brick house, turned office.

Other than the receptionist, the waiting area was empty. Soon the lawyer emerged from the hallway, her heels clicking on the hardwood floor as she approached Chuck with her hand extended. She was tall and slender with the poise of a model, and directed us to her office, which didn't match her feminine attributes at all. Everything from the brown leather chairs to the stuffed deer head starring down at me, screamed male.

After we were seated, Chuck went straight to the point. He told her about my parents' disapproval of our marriage, what he understood about the legal age difference between the two states, and how we needed advice on how to prevent my parents from legally interfering once we were married.

"Well, you're right about the age difference between the two states, and I can tell you, there's little anyone can do once you two are married, especially if twenty-four hours have passed, and the marriage has been consummated." She leaned forward, folded her hands upon the big mahogany desk. “However, you, Mr. Mathews, will need a parent’s signature, since you’re not twenty-one yet. The law requires you both to show a certified birth certificate, and you’ll each need to have a blood test. The test is not any different from what the state of Mississippi requires, so you could have it done at a Health Department there and bring a copy of the results with you.”

Once she answered all our questions, we thanked her for her time, and Chuck paid for her services.

When we stepped out of the building, he turned to me. “Do you feel better now?”

I shook my head. “Do you? Didn’t you hear her? You have to be twenty-one.”

“That’s not a problem. I’ll tell my father, and he’ll come with us.”

“Oh, no, you won’t! What if he goes straight to my parents?”

“My father may have his faults, but he’s not like yours. He and I are close. When I ask him, he’ll be happy for both of us. He and Mother always knew we’d get married someday.”

“They know about us?”

“Yes. Now can we go get something to eat? I’m starving.”

“Wait.” My feet remained firmly planted. “What does consummate mean?”

He snickered and placed an arm around my waist. “Come on. I’ll explain it later.”

The day had flown by, and now that I understood more about the legalities, I relaxed and enjoyed the trip back.

When we arrived on campus, Kyle drove to the far outer edge of the dorm parking lot. Becky, Chuck, and I got out. We said our good-byes and waited as Chuck got in the passenger seat. We waved and headed toward the dorm.

Becky came to a sudden stop. Her fingernails dug into my arm. "Morgan, there's your mom and dad."

"That's not funny." No sooner had the words escaped my mouth than I saw my parents driving toward us. I looked back where I'd last seen Chuck but knew he wouldn't be there. I froze and couldn't move. My mom got out of the car and walked slowly up to us. A tight smile strained her face. Her stare gripped me with fear.

"You just can't stay away from Chuck Mathews, can you?" She reached for my elbow then pulled my hand to her face. "Where did you get this?" She pointed at my left ring finger.

I could hardly make my voice answer. "Out of a box of Cracker Jacks."

My head jerked from the force of her blow. The side of my face burned.

She held me by both shoulders, forcing me to face her. "I asked you, where did you get the ring?"

I swallowed the bile in my mouth. "Out of a box of Cracker Jacks."

The next blow landed on my left ear. Ringing accompanied the severe pain. I didn't understand why the ring mattered, until I remembered the yellow plastic band resembled a wedding band. Chuck had told me next time it'd be the real thing.

She drew her hand back to slap me again, when I heard Becky's shrill voice. "Honestly Mrs. Selby, she did get it out of a box. It was a prize."

"You stay out of this, Becky Wilson. From the first time I laid my eyes on you, I've known what kind of girl you are."

She turned her attention to Dad who sat in the car watching, smoking a cigarette. "Get her in the car. I'll let Mrs. Henderson know she won't be staying here tonight."

Chapter 9

I'm *not* getting in that car! Think, Morgan! *God, please—give me courage.*

Dad opened the car door and placed one foot on the pavement. With his jaw jacked out, face red, and neck veins bulging, he glared at me. He took a puff from his cigarette, inhaled then blew the smoke out slowly, never breaking eye contact. "Get in."

I jumped at his harsh demand. My heart pounded, sending the sound of blood swooshing through both ears. I swallowed and attempted to steady my voice. "No."

In one quick motion, he stood, thumped the cigarette from his hand, and slammed a fist against the top of the car. "What did you say to me?"

"I'm…not leaving here." Teeth chattering. Unable to hold eye contact. Fear once again overruled my fleeting moment of courage.

He stalked closer. "You better not ever tell me no again." He reached for my shoulder, grabbed a handful of material, and snatched me forward, bringing our faces close. His tobacco breath made me gag.

"Walk," he growled. "Or I'll drag you."

My legs were like rubber. They kept wanting to collapse, but somehow I managed to get to the car. My brother, Wayne, sat in the backseat. Some girl I'd never seen before was with him.

"You're gonna regret your actions, girl." Dad's voice was quieter now, but still filled with the promise of pain. "I'm gonna make you remember this night for the rest of your life. Whatever it takes, I'll make sure Chuck Mathews is a thing of the past."

He opened the front passenger door, grasped my neck, and shoved me inside. I fell sprawling across the front seat.

"Sit down!"

I scooted into a sitting position.

He slammed the door, walked around, and got in behind the wheel.

As Dad drove toward the dorm's front entrance, Becky stood rooted to the sidewalk, eyes wide. She splayed her thumb and pinkie finger, and held them to her face as if talking on the phone. Was she trying to tell me she'd call for help? Call Chuck? Hope stirred, but quickly fizzled. Chuck and Kyle had left for Jackson, to pick up a car for Kyle's sister. He wouldn't be home for hours. It didn't matter. Neither he, nor anyone else, could help me now.

Mom came out of the dorm as Dad pulled up. She got in the car, pinning me between her and Dad. "We should've known better than to let you stay on campus." She pushed the button to raise the passenger window. "We'll have to make a trip back up here next week and get your things. As far as I'm concerned, you can forget about college. You can get a job and live at home until you turn twenty-one."

When I'm eighteen, I'm gone and you'll never see me again. The words played over in my mind in an attempt to hang onto sanity.

For the next several miles, no one uttered a word. Dad *would* make good on his promise. The physical wounds would heal, no matter how bad he beat me. But the emotional wounds worried me. They were already too deep. I'd experienced what life could be like with Chuck and friends. The hope that kept me alive was fading fast.

A car passed and a small child in the backseat waved and smiled. Curious thoughts ran through my mind. What kind of life did she have? Did her parents love and protect her? Were they proud of her?

Dad slowed and turned in at a convenience store. Mom needed a carton of milk for "the pain in her stomach". Dad offered to get it, but she ignored him and went into the store alone.

He lit another cigarette. "I hope you're happy. She'll suffer for weeks with her ulcer because of this unnecessary stress. We have you to thank for that, don't we?" His Masonic ring thumped against the back of my head. Searing pain brought tears to my eyes. "Don't we?"

"Yes, sir." I rubbed my scalp and stared at the floorboard, feeling no remorse for any discomfort my mom might feel. I knew this routine all too well. A game she played for sympathy and control.

"You'll apologize when she gets back in the car. And you better pray she doesn't end up in the hospital because of this."

"Yes, sir."

#

Once inside my parents' house, I asked and was given permission to use the bathroom. I locked the door and knelt beside the tub. *Lord, why? If I only knew why—*

Someone tapped on the door.

"Just a minute." I sprang to my feet, flushed the toilet, and ran water at the sink, stalling, pretending to wash my hands.

When I opened the door, instead of my mom, the unknown girl entered and closed the door behind her. She wasn't any taller than me. Her hair was brown and straight, her eyes green. "Wayne won't let anything happen to you," she stated. "He's in there talking to your dad now."

"Wayne? He couldn't stop him even if he wanted to. Who are you? How do you know my brother?"

Before she could answer, Mom pushed the door open. "What are you two doing in here?" She didn't wait for an answer. "Kay, I've moved your things to the bedroom next to ours. I'm going to have to ask you to wait there while we take care of this matter with Morgan."

Mom turned her gaze to me. "Your dad's in the kitchen waiting for you."

My mind whirled, and my legs shook as I walked slowly out of the room, down the hall, into the kitchen. I waited by the cabinet edge until Dad acknowledged me.

He remained seated at the table with my brother rather than leading the way to where I'd surely receive my punishment, a room on the opposite end of the house from Kay. The room. Instead, he pointed to a chair and ordered me to sit.

"You know what you deserve for your behavior tonight, and I've never been a man to go back on my word. But your brother asked us to consider Kay's presence in our home. He also feels it's important for you to continue your education. Your mother and I disagree, but frankly, I'm tired of putting up with you. Let me make one thing clear." He leaned forward and stuck his finger in my face. "You better hear and understand what I'm saying."

Mom walked by, drawing my attention. Dad's hand caught me unaware. The impact snapped my head to the side. "Look at me," he demanded. "If you're determined, we can't keep you from wallowing with trash, but we can stop you from ever setting foot in this home again. Tomorrow morning, first thing, I want you out of this house. For good. Do you understand?"

Was my mind working properly? Did I hear him correctly? I swallowed hard. "Yes, sir."

"Don't plan on coming back here until you've made up your mind who's more important—your family or Chuck Mathews. You keep hanging around that no good boy and you're dead as far as we're concerned. The choice is yours."

Mom chimed in, "We've helped you all we intend to. If you decide to go back to Midway, or drop out of college and get a job, it doesn't matter to us. Your father and I are through providing. We're not going to help you in any form or fashion—not anymore."

Yeah, right! Did they really think they'd helped me these last two months?

"You can thank your brother for saving your hide."

How? I'd never known anyone, other than Mom, capable of changing Frank Selby's mind. I searched Wayne's eyes for answers. His blank expression gave no clues.

"Thank you." My voice trembled.

Dad snapped his fingers and pointed toward the door. "Don't let me see or hear from you again tonight, or I'll forget we have company. Now get out of my sight."

I stood and drudged my way to my old bedroom, tears running down my face. I shoved a fist in my mouth to muffle the anguished sobs I couldn't hold. *Thank you, God, for protecting me tonight.* I repeated the prayer several more times. I'd witness a miracle. God had used an unknown girl and my brother as His instruments.

Even after my body began to relax, my mind wouldn't. I knew my parents well enough to know this sudden change of heart wouldn't last. I wanted to leave but couldn't. Not before morning, or they'd see my action as an act of defiance. But I had to come up with a plan.

Around midnight, I opened the bedroom door. No lights, no noise. The closest phone hung on the kitchen wall. We'd always said Mom could hear a spider walk across the floor, so making my phone call without getting caught would be difficult. In the dark, I counted each hole on the rotary phone, and I dialed Janet's number. Carefully placing a finger in what I hoped was the correct slot, I moved it clockwise and slowly took it back to its original spot. When her phone began ringing, I slipped into the utility room and closed the door on the cord.

"Hello?"

"Mrs. Barnes, this is Morgan," I whispered, my hand cupped the bottom of the phone by my mouth. "Can you hear me?"

"Morgan, is that you?"

In the background, I heard Mr. Barnes asking her what was wrong.

"Mrs. Barnes, I'm sorry to be calling so late, but could I speak to Janet?"

"Honey, Janet's been in bed for hours—we all have. Can you call back in the morning?"

"No. Mrs. Barnes, please. It's important. I need to talk with her tonight."

"Morgan, where are you?"

"At my parents."

"Just a minute."

The sound of the phone hitting a hard surface clattered through the line. I leaned against the washing machine and rubbed my aching temples.

"Morgan? What's wrong?" Janet rasped.

"I'm at my parents. Can you come get me in the morning and take me back to school?"

"What time?"

"Mom and Dad should be gone by eight."

"I'll be there by ten after. Are you okay? Did your dad—"

"I've got to go." I hung up the phone and returned to my bed. Before I pulled the covers in place, a scratching noise drew my attention. I didn't move. The sound came again, a distinct pattern of someone scratching on the screen. I sprang from the bed, tiptoed to the window, and opened it.

Chuck stared back at me.

"I didn't think you'd ever wake up. I've been out here for over ten minutes, wondering if you were in another room…or worse." His voice cracked. "Becky had half the town looking for me. She called everyone. Are you okay? How bad…?"

"I'm okay. They didn't… Dad didn't…"

He used his pocketknife to unhook the screen. "Come on, I'm getting you out of here."

"No." I explained about Kay and Wayne and told him what Dad said. "As long as Wayne's girlfriend is here, I don't think they'll do anything. Janet will come in the morning and take me back to Midway."

"You're leaving tonight."

"It's late, Chuck. Where would we go? The dorm is locked. I can't go to your grandmother's with you. And if we get caught together this time of night, nobody will be able stop Dad."

He dropped the screen on the ground and held his hands up for me. "I won't let him hurt you. Come on."

Dad's hunting dogs went crazy, barking and howling.

"Chuck, you've got to get out of here before the dogs wake Mom and Dad. I escaped severe punishment once tonight, it won't happen a second time. I'll call you at work tomorrow once I'm back at school. Thank Becky for me when you see her."

"You may see her before I do. She's still at Midway."

"She is?"

"Morgan, please don't stay here."

"Someone's up. Please, you have to leave."

"All right. I'm going. But remember, I'm a phone call away."

Footsteps shuffled down the hall. Then a light spilled under my door. I closed the window and scrambled back into bed.

The door opened, and footsteps entered my room. I tried hard to control my breathing, to lie perfectly still. I didn't dare peek. After what seemed like an eternity, whoever it was finally closed the door behind them.

#

The next morning, by seven forty-five, my parents left for work. I dressed without showering and called Janet.

Neither Wayne nor Kay had come out of their rooms yet, and I sure wasn't going to hang around until they did. I walked out of the house and waited at the end of the county road. God willing, I wouldn't be back.

Chapter 10

Around ten thirty Saturday morning, I walked into the dorm lobby relieved to be back in its familiar, protected environment.

Mrs. Henderson looked up from a stack of papers, pulled her glasses off, and allowed them to dangle on her chest by a gold chain. "Morgan, I'm surprised to see you…I thought… Did you have a nice visit?" She gazed beyond me, toward the parking lot. "Are you by yourself?"

I didn't feel like making small talk. Hungry, exhausted, and in need of a shower, I politely answered her last question and asked one of my own. "Have you seen Becky?"

"Not this morning, but she was here last night." She donned her glasses, picked up the logbook, and slowly shook her head. "She hasn't signed out."

I excused myself and went to find my friend. She wasn't in her room or in the shower. Probably at breakfast.

I entered my room and gathered clean clothes and items I needed to wash away yesterday's grim. But first, I needed to call Chuck's workplace.

Mr. Fisher answered, "Fisher Appliance."

Normally I would've tried to disguise my voice, but what did it matter? He's out on a service call was the response I expected. He's not here today, wasn't.

After a quick shower, I headed back downstairs to tape a note on Becky's door. I made it halfway down the hall when she called, "Morgan, wait up."

We hugged for a brief moment. "Becky, I'm so sorry for the hurtful things Mom said to you and for all the problems I've caused."

"I don't give a hoot what your mother thinks of me. She's the one who should be concerned about what people think of her. I've never seen anyone slapped so hard. Are you okay? Did they, you know, hurt you?"

"No. Yes, but not in the way you're thinking. Not with a belt."

We walked into her room and relaxed on her bed. I explained what happened after my parents got me home. "I expected the worst. It was pretty remarkable the way things worked out. A miracle."

"Why did you get in the car with your parents?"

"What choice did I have?"

Becky shrugged. "I don't know, but I never would've gone with them."

Heat rose from my neck to my face. She didn't understand. How could she? I hated myself for not having the courage to take a stand. There was no way I could explain how fear cripples. How I felt like a cracked vase, fragile, filled with hope that seeped away like an elusive dream.

Becky snapped her fingers in front of my face. "Morgan!"

I glanced around the room. "What?"

"You're tripping. Where'd you go?"

I ran my hand across my forehead trying to regain my earlier wits. I needed Chuck.

"Becky, would you do me a favor and call Fisher Appliance? When I called earlier, Mr. Fisher told me Chuck wasn't at work, but I didn't think to ask why."

"Sure, where's the number?"

I reached into my pocket, removed the slip of paper with the number, and handed it over.

Becky placed the call. Her conversation with Mr. Fisher didn't provide any more answers than we already had, so I decided to have her call Chuck's grandmother.

Becky glanced at me as she hung up the phone then took a deep breath. "Now don't get upset, but Chuck quit his job this morning."

"What? What do you mean he quit his job?"

She removed her hand from the payphone. "That's all his grandmother said. He gave his notice and took the rest of the day off. She doesn't know where he is."

We returned to Becky's room. I wrung my hands and tried to make sense out of the latest information, but my mind couldn't untangle all the unanswered questions.

"Hey, why don't we go get something to eat?" Becky grabbed me by my elbows and gave a light jerk. "Come on, Morgan, you can't sit around here all day. You won't do anything but work yourself into a tailspin."

"Thanks, Becky, but I'm too exhausted. Things are not making sense. Maybe I'll go to my room and lie down for a while. Not sleep, but rest. Come get me if you hear anything."

#

I felt a light nudge on my shoulder before hearing Becky's voice. "Morgan, I need to talk to you. Wake up."

Sliding my legs off the bed, I sat up rubbing my eyes. "Have you heard from Chuck?"

"Not a word, and it's almost four thirty, but I did get in touch with Kyle. He hasn't seen Chuck and didn't know anything about him quitting his job. But he'll see what he can find out and call us back at six thirty."

"It's not like him, Becky. Wouldn't you think that since I can't call him, he'd call me?"

"I don't know, but you can't sit in this room all night, and neither of us has a car. We have no choice but to wait to hear from Kyle. Meanwhile, let's get something to eat. You haven't had anything all day."

The cafeteria hadn't started serving yet, so we went to Eddie's. I ate like a starving bird dog, not only from hunger, but I didn't want to miss Kyle's call.

As we walked back to the dorm, Becky tried to distract me by pointing out how beautiful the yellow and brown leaves were swirling around the ground. "At this rate, the trees will be naked in another month. And the air, can you smell it? The scent of autumn."

I partially paid attention to her ramblings.

No sooner had the lobby doors closed behind us, and I stood stock still, gaping. Chuck and Mrs. Henderson sat across from one another in matching wing-backed chairs. They chatted away, completely unaware of our entrance.

Becky finally broke the silence. "Chuck, what are you doing?"

"Yes, what are you doing here?" I wanted to scream, but managed to maintain a calm tone. Did he know who he was talking to?

Chuck rose. "Hey, girls, I decided you two wouldn't be gone long." His smile broadened. "So, Mrs. Henderson and I have been getting to know one another better."

"Yes." She stood and faced Chuck with an extended hand, her expression unreadable. "It's nice to have met you. I enjoyed our conversation. I'll leave you young people to enjoy your evening."

She looked directly at me. "Morgan, don't forget to sign out if you plan on leaving the campus."

Chuck spoke, "We won't be going any farther than my car."

Her eyes shifted from me to Becky. "Well, I'll be in my apartment if you girls need me."

She gathered a tray with cups and saucers then headed toward her quarters.

"Thank you," I muttered, before glaring at Chuck.

I didn't speak another word until her door closed. "What are you doing? Where have you been all day? Why haven't you called? What were you and Mrs. Henderson talking about?"

Becky cleared her throat. "I've got some homework to do. I'm glad you're okay, Chuck. Holler at me later, Morgan." She walked away. Her footsteps soon faded in the empty hallway.

Chuck opened the lobby door. "I thought we could talk in the car."

Outside, when I was sure no one could hear, I whirled toward him. "What is wrong with you? Where have you been? Your grandmother said you quit your job. And then I walk in the lobby and find you and the dorm mother having a tea party! What's going on?"

He grinned and laced his fingers with mine. "It wasn't tea. It was coffee."

"What?"

"I said, we had—"

"Who cares what she served." I snatched my hand from his. "Have you lost your mind?"

Chuck leaned over and planted a quick, but firm, kiss on my

lips. "I've always loved that feisty personality."

I stomped my foot against the pavement. "I mean it, Chuck."

"Okay." He chuckled and backed away. "But let's go sit in the car and talk."

We walked in silence. He held the passenger door for me. I sat and waited for him to settle in the driver's seat.

He shifted his body to face me, laid his hand across my shoulder, and rubbed my neck. "When no one answered the phone at Janet's house this morning, I figured you had to be on your way back here as planned. I called her house again at nine. No answer, so I left Greer and got here a little after eleven. When I called your floor and didn't get anyone, I phoned Mrs. Henderson. She told me you'd been here since ten thirty."

I breathed deep and released the air slowly. "That still doesn't answer the question of where you've been. But first, I want to know what you said to Mrs. Henderson."

"The truth. I explained if she felt the need to notify your parents about us dating, then she should know about the physical abuse you've suffered for years."

"You didn't?"

"Yes, I did. I hate it when your parents mistreat you. But they know about us now, and I'm glad. Now Mrs. Henderson knows about them. We love each other, Morgan. We're through hiding. We can get married without them interfering."

"No. Don't ever think they'd give up so easily. My parents aren't through with me, and they'll never allow us to get married. If Kay and my brother hadn't been there last night, things would've turned out so different. *You don't know them.*"

He reached over and softly kissed my cheek, then my lips. "It's okay, Morgan. I'm here now. Not just for tonight, but every night. I rented a small house not too far from the campus, and I spent the day looking for a job. I start in two weeks."

"What kind of job?"

"Doing the same thing I did for Mr. Fisher, repairing appliances. Meanwhile, I'll commute from here to finish my two weeks for Mr. Fisher. But I don't ever want you to have to face your parents alone again."

I wanted to believe his words and loved him even more for wanting to protect me. *God, if only it could be true.* I slid into his arms and enjoyed the love and comfort they provided. His touch, smell, and kisses sent waves of tremors throughout my body. But then Dad's threats of harm to Chuck resurfaced. It would take a miracle for us to have the life I'd been praying for.

Chapter 11

Gusty wind greeted Becky and me as we walked down the church steps. Our hair blew in multiple directions. Dark, low hanging clouds obscured the sun, and an occasional raindrop fell.

Becky forced her Bible into her already overstuffed purse. "We better run, or we're going to get wet."

"Looks like it." I wrapped my sweater snug around me as we sprinted across the street toward the campus. "Can you believe neither of us remembered an umbrella?"

"What I really can't believe," she shouted over her shoulder, "is Chuck picked such a nasty day to move."

"I sure hope he and Kyle are already at the house and they've gotten everything unloaded."

Becky held out her palm as the number of drops increased. "Come on." She picked up the pace. "Before we get drenched."

Tree limbs began to sway with the force of the wind as rain pelted us at a forty-five-degree angle. By the time we made it inside the dorm, my hair, clothes, and shoes were soaked.

Becky wasn't in much better shape. Black mascara dribbled down both cheeks, and her hair plastered to her head. I had to choke back a giggle.

"What's so funny?"

"You." I erupted into snorts and cackles. "You should see your face."

She mopped clingy wet hair from her eyes as we studied our reflections in the mirror hanging in the entranceway. Four sullied eyes, squinting through black smudged faces, stared back at us. Complete silence gave way to piercing squeals of our own mockery.

The lighthearted mood was soothing medicine.

As we headed down the hall, I asked, "You're still going, right?"

"To see the house? Sure. But first I'll need to change clothes and do something with this hair and face."

"Good." I peeled off the heavy cardigan and draped it over my arm. "After I get myself cleaned up and hear from Chuck, I'll come get you."

#

While I ran a comb through my wet hair, my excitement intensified at the thought of seeing the house Chuck and I would soon share as husband and wife. When the phone rang, I sprinted out of my room and down the hall, eager to hear his voice. "Hello?"

"Morgan?"

My smile vanished. "Yes, ma'am."

"Where have you been?" Mom spoke in cadence.

I shook my head. *This can't be happening.* "I've been at church."

"You've been at church all morning?"

"I left here around ten thirty. Why? What's wrong?" I tightened my fist, angry with myself for asking the questions that played right into her hands. I held my breath, not wanting to hear the ugly remarks sure to follow.

"You left this house over twenty-four hours ago—without

saying a word to anyone—and you want to know what's wrong? What's wrong with *you*, Morgan?"

"Dad told me to leave...so I left." I began to have difficulty breathing and controlling my shaky voice.

"Don't you get smart with me, Morgan Selby."

"I-I'm not. I don't know what you want me to say." I not only felt my heart pounding in my chest, but also heard each rapid beat.

"According to Wayne, you left yesterday before he woke. What time did you leave and with whom?"

I tightened my grip on the phone. Still, it shook with every tremor of my hand. I moved it further from my ear to stop the receiver from striking me while I tried to form my answer. I didn't want to involve Janet and her mother. Mrs. Barnes, if pushed, wouldn't have any qualms telling Mom what she thought about her. History had proven that.

"What difference does it make how I got here?"

"Don't you dare. Do I need to call your father to the phone?"

I clutched the topaz necklace around my neck. "No, ma'am."

"I know Chuck didn't work yesterday. Did he come to this house?"

How did she know this stuff? "No, ma'am."

"Then who drove you back?"

I hesitated.

"Who! Answer me."

"Janet did."

"I better not find out Chuck Mathews stepped foot in this house or anywhere on our property. And, Morgan, you can be assured, I'll be talking with Mrs. Barnes."

She hung up.

I returned the phone to its base and trudged toward my room. I'd made it over halfway when the phone rang again.

I wanted to scream. Why won't she leave me alone?

Remembering it could be Chuck, I headed back to the phone room. *Please, God, let it be him.*

I lifted the receiver and held it to my ear without saying a word, nor did I plan to without knowing who was on the other end.

"Hello?"

Chuck's voice soothed my unraveled nerves. "Hi. I'm sorry about not answering, but I wanted to make sure it was you. Where are you?"

"I'm at Eddie's. What's going on?"

"Mom called a few minutes ago." I described our conversation and her mood.

"Morgan, I want you to pack some extra clothes to bring in case we get back to the dorm tonight and your parents are there."

"You don't think that'll happen, do you?"

"No, but if they show up, we'll have a plan. Don't let them get to you."

"Becky's coming with me."

"That's fine," he assured me. "We'll have more than enough food. But don't answer the phone if it rings again, okay?"

"All right, but hurry."

"Try not to worry. I'll be there in a few minutes."

I ran back to my room and corrected the rain-damaged hair and makeup. Then I shoved pajamas and some personal items in a tote bag, grabbed a dress—hanger and all—and left to get Becky."

She eyed the bag. "What's going on?"

"Mom called—"

"Are they here…on their way?" She motioned for me to finish zipping her dress. "I'll die if your parents show up again. Your parents are crazy—no offense—but I won't watch a repeat of what happened Friday without calling the police."

She talked tough, but I knew Becky was afraid. We both were. "Don't panic." Words spoken for my benefit more than hers. "They're not here, but hopefully Chuck and Kyle are. Come on. I'll explain on the way."

By the time we made it to the lobby, the guys were pulling up to the front door. Chuck jumped out with an umbrella and escorted us to the car. He took the tote bag from me and placed it on the floorboard after I slid across the backseat.

Kyle navigated his bright yellow Camaro out of the parking lot and drove a short distance to a simple white cottage in dire need of fresh paint. Dirt peeked through scant patches of dead grass. Even the one lonely tree stood contorted and naked of its leaves. The only thing thriving was the row of hedges with spindly branches greedily fighting for equal space.

"I hope you're not disappointed. There's not a lot to choose from this time of year in a college town. It's only temporary." His tender expression assured me. "We'll find something better this summer."

"Are you kidding?" I opened the car door and tugged at his hand, sure the two of us would be happy living anywhere. "Come on. Let's go see the inside."

We approached through the front door where boxes and suitcases cluttered the dark oak floor. Touring the house took only minutes. Bare necessities furnished the rooms. A blue Naugahyde sofa and matching chair in the living room. A yellow Formica chrome table with four padded chairs in the kitchen. And only a double mattress and bedsprings sat on a metal frame in the bedroom. But the unpretentious surroundings represented much more than material items. A sense of hope and possibilities washed over me. Flashes of a life full of peace, contentment, and love danced in my mind.

Chuck eased behind me, wrapped his arms around my waist, and pulled me back against his body. "It's not much to look at, but it'll do for a start, won't it?"

I leaned my head against his shoulder. "The house is perfect. By the time we get everything cleaned, you won't recognize the place. A few plants, pictures, and throw rugs with splashes of red will give it that warm, cozy feeling it's lacking. You'll see. All it needs is a little TLC."

His laughter vibrated the air. "What's that, time and lots of cash?"

"Wherever we live." I faced him. "If we're together, it'll be home."

He ran a gentle finger down my nose before gathering me in his arms and covering my lips with his.

All of life's troubles faded away, replaced by love. Love I'd never known or thought to be possible.

#

After lunch, the four of us dusted and scrubbed every room before unpacking a hodgepodge of used household items from pans and sheets, to mismatched Melmac plates and Pyrex bowls.

I removed a small sewing kit from one of the boxes. "Where did you get all this stuff?"

"When you have two married sisters *and* a grandmother like mine, you only have to let your needs be known. Mother helped out, too."

Becky and I had finished organizing the kitchen when Kyle came in with a deck of cards. "Anyone for a game of Rook?"

I grinned at Becky. "Girls against the guys?"

"Yeah, right. Like you two stand a chance. Come on, Chuck. We're going to teach these girls how to play cards."

Becky reached in the cupboard and set four glasses on the counter. "I'll fix us all a Coke while you shuffle, Mr. Big Shot."

The afternoon proved both enjoyable and productive. By seven, we'd achieved our goal of making the house livable, and the guys had beaten the girls two games out of three. But knowing the doors at the dorm would be locked by eight, we had to break it up.

Chuck expressed his doubts that my parents would be waiting for us, but after Friday's escapade, we decided to take extra precautions. I couldn't help but feel more than a little apprehensive, but my bag of clothing and the dress waited in his bedroom closet in the event my parents ever presented themselves as surprise visitors.

When we arrived, Kyle turned into the dorm parking lot and drove slowly. We scanned the area before driving through each section. Becky volunteered to go inside and check with the girl at the front desk and soon came running back to the car where the three of us stood.

"No messages and no visitors."

Chuck wrapped his arms around me. "I don't know what time I'll make it back tomorrow. Remember it's a two-hour drive, but it's only for a couple of weeks."

He removed a slip of paper from his shirt pocket and handed it to me, along with a key.

"This is the name of a friend of mine and his dorm phone number. He has a car and the address to the house. I've told him about us and the problems with your parents. He's more than willing to help. He said to call him anytime. Make sure Becky has this information also."

I tried to enjoy the comfort of Chuck's embrace but couldn't relax and not continually cheek over my shoulder. "I better go." I stood on my tiptoes to kiss him good night. "I'm glad you're going to be close by."

"Everything's going to work out, Morgan."

We kissed a few more times, then said good night. Before walking away, I reached for Kyle's hand. "Thanks for all your help."

"Not a problem. I'd do just about anything for you two." He leaned down and hugged me and whispered in my ear, "Take care of him, Morgan. I may not be around much longer to keep the dope in line."

I searched his eyes. "Why do you say that? You're not going anywhere."

"I'm leaving after Christmas. I've joined the Army."

"Why, Kyle? With Vietnam in the mess it's in, why?"

"My father and grandfather joined the Army at a younger age than me. I guess it's past time for me to follow in their footsteps. It's what some men have to do."

I stood there, unable to find the right words. My heart ached as I considered the horrific scenes depicted on the nightly news.

"You two girls better get in there," Chuck kissed the back of my neck, "before Mrs. Henderson has my scalp."

Becky and I headed for the dorm. Within inches of reaching the door, I stopped and spun around, looking at a sea of empty cars.

"What is it, Morgan?"

"I don't know. It's the strangest thing, like someone's watching us."

Chapter 12

What a weekend. So many events made it difficult to comprehend the reality of it all. Totally exhausted, I climbed in bed immediately after bed checks. Paige turned out the lights and retired a few minutes later. After more than an hour of tossing, I forced all the negative occurrences aside and focused on the positive impact Chuck's recent changes would have on our lives. I'd finally begun to feel the onset of sleep when a faint squeak from the door hinges jarred me awake. I turned my head in the direction of the noise as a shadowy figure tiptoed toward me. Before I could reach for the lamp, Becky whispered my name.

"What are you doing?" I hissed back. "Don't you know if you get caught out of your room after hours, we're both in trouble?"

"We need to talk."

If Paige woke during the quiet commotion, she never said a word. I pushed the covers back and followed Becky out of the room to the lounge. I switched on the overhead light only long enough to find the table lamp and turn it on. Becky sat beside me on the brown corduroy couch.

"Okay, what's wrong?"

"It's Mimi Clair." Becky folded her arms across her chest. "She recognized Kyle's Camaro tonight. Apparently, she'd gone out to her car to get something and saw us. But it gets worse. She also saw you kissing Chuck."

"You've got to be kidding me. That's great. Maybe I should take out an ad in the *Bradford County Herald* and let the whole town of Greer know about me and Chuck. Not that I'm ashamed or have anything to hide—not anymore. But if people start asking Mom a lot of questions, it could have the same effect as poking a hornet's nest."

"She didn't get a good look at Chuck, but she's convinced it was him. You know how insistent Mimi can get. Her curiosity won't go away without some kind of answer." Becky wrapped the drawstring from her pajama bottoms around her finger. "We got in a snip because I wouldn't blab."

"I'm sorry, Becky. Since you agreed to be my maid of honor, life's become one giant headache for you, hasn't it? I promise, if you want to back out, I'll understand."

"Forget it. I wouldn't miss this wedding for anything. Don't worry about me. It's you I'm concerned about. If Mimi Clair finds out about Chuck, the phone lines will burn right off the poles. I love her, but she cannot keep her mouth shut to save anybody's life."

I laughed, visualizing cables blazing. "Yep, South Central Bell would have their hands full for sure."

Her eyes widened. "We could always make up some fake boyfriend."

"No...it's not like my parents don't already know about Chuck. Besides, now that he lives in town, he'll be coming by the dorm during the week. Mimi's bound to find out sooner or later. I might as well tell her. But we've got to make sure she never finds out about us getting married."

"She won't." Becky assured me. "Oh, she'll ask all kind of questions, marriage plans included, but we'll downplay it."

"I've got Music Theory tomorrow morning at eight. I'd like to tell her before then and get it over with. How about we meet in the lobby at six thirty and go to breakfast?"

"I don't know if she'll want to go to breakfast that early. What should I tell her?"

"The truth. That I need to talk to her."

"All right, but what if she refuses to go?"

"We'll worry about that tomorrow. Right now, we've got to get back to our rooms before we get caught and written up. I'll go first and check the halls. Remember, if you hear or see somebody, head to the bathroom."

#

On the way to the cafeteria the next morning, Mimi Claire only spoke when questioned, and then responded in a stoic manner. When I looked to Becky for an answer, she shrugged. The smell of coffee and bacon greeted us when we arrived, but my stomach quivered at the thought of having anything more than lightly buttered toast and milk. Mimi's silent treatment unnerved me.

After having our meal tickets punched, I chose a table by an east-facing window in hopes of a glorious sunrise possibly brightening the mood. Once seated, I started with the statement I'd practiced all morning, "Mimi, I understand you saw me with Chuck last night."

"I knew it!" Mimi glared at Becky. "Didn't I tell you?"

"I need this to stay between the three of us. I'd really appreciate it if you wouldn't say anything to anyone. Especially anyone from Greer."

"Oh, you can trust me, Morgan."

Mimi Clair rattled on for several minutes about how she'd always suspected Chuck and I might still be seeing one another. Then without warning, her smile disappeared. "Wait a minute." She spun toward Becky. "You knew all along, didn't you?" When Becky didn't respond, Mimi jerked her head my direction. "Why didn't you tell me before today?"

I opened my mouth and tried with all my might to come up with something intelligent. Something to douse Mimi's anger, but not one brilliant thought dislodged itself.

After another awkward moment, Becky took over and handled her like a pro. "You're such an honest person, Mimi. We hated to ask you to compromise your standards. Everyone knows how difficult it is for you to hold the truth inside."

By the time Becky completed her sugarcoated rendition, I had to make a conscious effort to close my mouth.

Mimi reached over and hugged Becky. "You're such a good friend…both of you. Y'all know me better than anyone."

When Mimi thanked us for the second time for being so thoughtful, I chewed on the tip of my thumbnail and avoided eye contact with either of them. Instead, I glanced at the wall clock. Seven twenty. *Close enough.* I gathered my books, excused myself, and left for class.

#

I'd planned on telling the rest of the girls about Chuck when we gathered in Jennifer's room, as usual, later that afternoon. But my day was hectic, and an unscheduled meeting of the majorettes to discuss Christmas uniforms caused me to get back to the dorm later than usual.

"Morgan Selby, you have a telephone call," the cry sounded before the stairway door closed behind me. Not wanting another confrontation with Mom, I waved at the girl calling my name.

"Wait, Carol." I hurried closer. "Did they say who was calling?"

"No, she didn't."

She! "I hate to ask you to do this, but would you take a message for me?"

"Sure. What do you want me to tell her?"

"Find out who it is and what they want. Tell 'em I'll call them back later."

I followed her back inside the phone room and lingered in the doorway as she picked up the receiver dangling by a metal cord.

"Can I take a message?" She nodded several times before responding. "I'll tell her. And you said your name is Janet?"

Janet! I reached for the phone. "Thanks, Carol. I'll take it."

"Janet, don't hang up. I'm sorry. I didn't know it was you. I was afraid it might be Mom. How are you?"

"Hey, girl. I'm fine. Listen, I've got something to tell you."

"Okay."

"Promise you won't get upset."

"You're scaring me, Janet. Just tell me."

"Mother had a hair appointment today, and your mother was there."

"Oh, no. What did Mom say to her?"

"She didn't say anything. It's what Mother overheard her telling the ladies at the salon."

As hard as I tried to control them, tremors shook my body. "What? Tell me. What did she hear?"

"Your mother has this crazy idea that you and Chuck plan to run off and get married in the next few weeks, as soon as you turn eighteen. And here's the really crazy part, supposedly, your parents have someone watching you."

"Watching me? What do you mean? They're *paying* someone to

watch me?"

"Mother never heard her say who. But the plan is to stop you, and if they can't, then they'll have the marriage annulled."

"How does she know? We've been so careful."

Janet squealed. "Oh, I can't believe it! You mean it's true?"

"Yes." My voice cracked, and tears began to roll down my face. "What do we do now? I don't know what to do anymore."

"Don't cry. Hang on a minute. Mother wants to talk to you."

Mrs. Barnes's calm, sweet voice vibrated over the line, "Morgan, I had Janet call so you'd know what your parents were up to. Honey, they apparently have no intention of allowing you and Chuck to marry, but that doesn't mean you can't."

When she paused, I brushed the tears away and wiped my runny nose with the back of my hand, then covered my mouth to try controlling the convulsive sobs.

"Listen, Morgan. Your mother might be bluffing, but in case she's not, wait her out. Meanwhile, make yourself visibly available. They can't watch you forever, and they can't afford to pay someone to do it for long. Everything will work out. I'm sorry, honey, but you needed to know. Are you going to be all right?"

"M-uh," I responded with uncontrollable spasms, still crying and gulping for air.

"We'll be praying for you, and if I hear anything else, I'll let you know. We love you."

I hung up the phone, unable to voice my thanks, and leaned against the concrete wall. A moment later, I slid to the floor, hugged my legs tight to my chest, buried my head in my arms, and wailed. For the first time since placing my trust in Christ, I couldn't pray. The words wouldn't come.

Someone touched my arm. "Are you all right?"

I didn't respond. I couldn't.

Sometime later, Becky's and Jennifer's voices washed over me and their hands lifted me under my arms. My legs wobbled like rubber, unable to hold me up. But with their assistance and encouragement, I made it back to my room. They sat with me in silence and supplied me with tissues until I regained some composure.

Jennifer spoke first. "Do you want to talk about it?"

"Not right now. Maybe later."

"How about some water or a Coke? It might make you feel better?"

I shook my head. "Thanks, Jennifer. I don't want anything."

Becky looked at her. "Why don't we let her rest for a while?"

Jennifer rose then glanced back. "The girls are all worried about you. What do you want us to tell them?"

"That I'm fine and I'll…I'm fine. You know, maybe a Coke would help. There's some money on my nightstand."

Jennifer left the room.

Becky stood, closed the door, and leaned against it. "Was it your mom on the phone?"

"No. But they know. I don't know how, but they know all about our plans."

She walked over and sat beside me. I quickly explained the phone conversation.

"I don't believe it. I think when she noticed Mrs. Barnes, your mother made up the whole thing. Oh, don't get me wrong, she probably suspects you and Chuck are thinking about marriage, but the only thing she knows for sure is Janet or her mother would call you. And they did. In a few weeks, you and Chuck will be married. Don't let her—" Becky held a finger to her lips and nodded toward the door.

"Hi, Mimi. What are you doing standing out in the hallway?"

Jennifer asked.

Becky sprang to her feet, walked across the room, and jerked the door open. "Mimi, how long have you been standing there?"

Jennifer edged around Becky and set a bag of chips on the desk. "Here you go." She handed a bottle to me.

I took the Coke, but my focus remained on Mimi. What had she heard? What would she tell?

Chapter 13

I've never been known for having a keen sense of direction, but I had to get away. There were too many prying questions. So even though Chuck wouldn't be home for a few hours, I decided to strike out on foot to try to find the cottage he'd rented for us.

The fading orange glow of the western sky may have matched the fall décor, but the chill hinted winter would soon take its place. A shiver ran down my spine. Not from the cool breeze sending colorful leaves swirling in the yards and down the streets like discarded confetti, but because I couldn't stop looking behind me…wondering. Was Mrs. Barnes right? Was someone watching me?

I spotted the house, ran the rest of the way, and used the key Chuck had given me. After turning on a few lights and adjusting the thermostat, I canvassed the refrigerator and cabinets for supper ideas, then busied myself making the bed and tidying the bathroom. Anything to help hurry time along.

At six, I started supper. It was my first time to cook on a gas stove, but that turned out to be the least of my problems. The cupboards held a mishmash of everything but the essentials. Without a mixer, potato masher, strainer, measuring cup, sharp knife, and only one boiler, preparing supper was more of a challenge than anticipated. Nothing looked or tasted right. The potatoes were lumpy, the country fried steak tough, the canned corn gummy, and the biscuits…a complete joke. I'd never used a packaged mix before, so I made them extra thick in case they didn't rise. Big mistake. When I last checked, they were half the size of grapefruit and growing.

Light splashed across the window as a car turned in the driveway. The soft purr of the engine I'd grown accustomed to hearing meant Chuck was home. I opened the door and welcomed him with a smile.

"Hey, babe. What a surprise." He leaned down and kissed me. "Something smells good."

"Smell's the only thing supper has going for it. There's not a knife in the house sharp enough to cut the meat. I'm afraid it'll just be potatoes, gravy, and bis—the bread!"

I ran to the kitchen, grabbed a hot-pad, and removed a pan holding four scorched cannonball-size biscuits. "I give up."

Chuck peered over my shoulder. "Just the way I like 'em." He led me to the table, sat, and pulled me onto his lap.

My gaze dropped to the floor. "This day has been so lousy. I wanted supper to be a surprise."

When he didn't respond, I turned. His eyes twinkled, his lips twitched, and then he burst into gales of laughter.

He wrapped his arms around me. "I'm not laughing at you. Honest."

I jumped to my feet. "You're making fun of me." Never mind the stove showcasing four of the largest briquets on record.

By the time Chuck stood in front of me, I couldn't contain my own amusement. We held one another and howled hysterically.

"We've got to stop it." I wiped the moisture from my eyes.

"This mess has to be cleaned up and me back at the dorm before eight. I'm afraid you'll have to settle for a peanut butter sandwich or a hamburger from Eddie's."

"Oh, no." He scooted a chair out and motioned for me to sit. "You cooked it. We're going to eat it." Still smiling, he joined me and gripped my hand. "And after we've blessed it, we'll tell each other about our day."

I closed my eyes and bowed my head, but my prayer had nothing to do with the pitiful meal before us.

"Amen." He gave my hand a squeeze and began dishing food on our plates. "You go first. What mischief have you and the girls gotten into today?"

"It's not about the girls...it's about my mother."

I started with the phone call from Janet and ended with Mimi Clair standing outside my door.

He reached for his glass of tea and took a drink. "Your parents don't give up easily, do they?"

"No, and they won't ever."

"Well, I think Becky's right. I see your mother as a chess player. Every move she makes studied and calculated to give her what she wants at any cost. Don't let it get to you." He pointed his fork at me. "Why aren't you eating?"

"But what if she has someone watching us? What if it's Mimi? Mimi might not do it deliberately, but you know how she loves to talk and how good my mom is at manipulating."

"I'm not worried about it. Let 'em do whatever they want. We're getting married."

"But what *if* somebody's watching? Like Mrs. Barnes said. They could be out there now for all I know."

Chuck leaned toward the window and flipped the curtain back. "I don't see anybody."

I punched his upper arm. "That's not funny."

"I'm sorry, Morgan, but one of these days, you're going to have to change all that fear into trust. It's like my grandmother says, 'If you worry, why pray, and if you pray, why worry.' There's no need to do both."

"You don't know my parents."

He paused, removed his checkbook from his pants pocket, opened it, and studied the calendar in front.

"What are you doing?"

He picked up a pencil and circled a date. "I say you tell the girls about us—including our marriage plans."

"Are you nuts? Even if Mimi isn't the one spying on me, she'll never be able to keep quiet about it."

He shrugged. "It doesn't matter."

I laid the fork with a bite of potato back on the plate. "What's that supposed to mean?"

"If...and that's a big if...your parents or someone else is watching us, then we'll give them something to gawk at and Mimi Clair something to talk about. We'll continue with our plans to get married November the fifteenth, as far as anyone knows." He moved the calendar for me to view and tapped the point of the pencil on the date he'd circled. "But, we'll change the date."

"To the twenty-sixth? That's so far away."

"I don't like it any better than you do, but listen, everyone will be expecting us to run off the fifteenth. But we'll stay close to the dorm—walking, sitting, holding hands." He winked. "Maybe even a little smooching. All in plain view. The next night, we'll do the same thing. When the girls ask, you can tell them we've had second thoughts, or we've temporarily postponed the wedding."

I picked up the checkbook. "The Tuesday before Thanksgiving?"

"Yes, and it's perfect. We'll go to Alabama and get married. You'll go back to the dorm that night and to classes the next morning. No one will suspect we're married. I'll pick you up at noon on Wednesday, and we'll leave town for a short honeymoon. By the time your parents find out, there won't be anything they can do about it. It's not exactly what I had in mind, but..."

I ran my thumbnail across my lower teeth. "I hate to postpone our wedding, but it might work."

Chuck glanced at his watch and scooted his chair from the table. "We've got to get going. It's ten till eight."

I sprang to my feet and snatched my purse off the counter. "We won't make it."

"You see, that's what I'm talking about. You're wound like an eight-day clock."

"The kitchen." A total wreck. "You haven't even finished eating, and we never had a chance to discuss *your* day."

"Don't worry about it. I've got the rest of the night to clean, and we can talk on the way."

Chuck pulled in front of the dorm with two minutes to spare.

Mrs. Henderson stood in the lobby. Keys in hand. "Cutting it a little close, aren't you, Morgan?"

"Yes, ma'am, but I made it."

Then I ran down the hall. Out of breath, I stopped at Becky and Mimi Clair's room, knocked, and waited. The last time I'd seen either one of them, all our emotions ran high. Becky opened the door.

"Where's Mimi?"

"Taking a shower, I guess. Why?"

After explaining the change of plans, I asked, "Do you think you could rush her along and meet me in my room in fifteen minutes?"

"I'll try."

When I reached the third floor, I went door to door and requested my friends' presence for a quick meeting. I found Becky and Mimi Clair waiting with Paige in my room. By eight twenty, the rest of the girls arrived.

I closed the door, took a deep breath, and faced them. "Remember the roses and the secret admirer?"

Paula clapped. "You finally met him."

"Not exactly. There is no secret admirer. At least not to anyone but y'all. His name is Chuck. We've known each other for four years."

The girls swapped looks and murmured.

"I didn't tell you because I was afraid. My parents don't approve of him. They made it almost impossible for us to see one another after our first year of dating. Anyway, they found out about him this past weekend."

"Why don't they like him?"

"I don't know, Ann."

"They had to give you a reason," she continued.

"When they first broke us up, I wasn't given a reason. As time passed, it became a matter of, 'because I said so.' But he's the nicest guy any girl could ever hope for, and I love him."

Jennifer grabbed my arm. "When do we get to meet him?"

"Soon, but I have something else to tell you." I scanned the room and hated not telling them the whole truth. "We're getting married."

Squeals, laughter, and hugs disrupted the semi-calm atmosphere.

After Paige took control and hushed the girls, I continued, "We're getting married November fifteenth. I wish all of you could be there, but we're not having a church wedding. We're eloping. If my parents find out, they'll try to stop me. Possibly have our marriage annulled."

"Can they do that?" Wendy asked.

I bit my lip and nodded.

Mimi walked up to me. "Do you think they'd try?"

"They might. According to the phone call I got today, that's their plan."

Mimi spun and scowled at Becky. "I knew there was more to the phone call than you said."

Becky shook her head. "It doesn't matter. We can talk about it later."

"I'm afraid we'll all have to talk about it another time. It's almost nine," Paige announced.

After a few more questions and further congratulations, the girls left for their own rooms. Except for Mimi Clair. "You said y'all were eloping, but you didn't say where."

"No, I didn't."

"Can't you tell me? I won't say a thing. My lips are sealed." She made her signature gesture of holding an invisible key to her tightly closed lips and turning it. "Come on, Morgan. Your secret is safe with me."

Chapter 14

What a hectic week. With an English paper due, a test on Western Civilization to study for, plus the hours I put in at the front desk, my afternoons and nights disappeared. I missed socializing with Chuck and the girls.

Chuck continued to put in twelve-hour days between work and traveling, and only managed to stop by each evening for a brief visit.

Wednesday it seemed I'd hardly closed my eyes when my alarm woke me. I kept slapping at the thing, but it kept blaring, it's piercing sound deafening.

"Fire!" Paige jumped out of bed and opened the door.

The place had erupted into complete chaos. Girls collided with each other as they ran through the hall. Some panic stricken, others laughing as if they enjoyed the excitement and freedom to be out and about, without the threat of being written up.

"It's all a hoax," someone shouted. "Everyone go back to bed."

"Somebody shut the thing off!" another voice shouted.

"Is it a drill, you think?"

"I don't think so." Paige slipped her arms into her black corduroy jacket. "Not this time of night."

Finally, Mrs. Henderson's voice screeched over the intercom, "This is not a drill. I repeat: this is not a drill. Everyone leave the building immediately. Monitors, clear the rooms and hallways, now!"

Within minutes, the third floor stood empty of girls. The other monitor and I joined everyone outside. We gathered in the cool, damp night and waited for the city fire department to give the all clear. The longer the wait, the hotter the tempers. It didn't help when the dorm mother called for repeat bed checks after we were allowed back inside. The absence of two girls justified her decision. By morning, rumor had it that the missing girls had fallen asleep in a car and were unaware of the orders given to return to our rooms. It was also determined that someone pulled the fire alarm. No one confessed to the prank, but we all felt punished when the dean of women scheduled a mandatory in-service the following day.

I don't think anyone looked forward to the end of the week as much as I did. I'd barely walked out of my last class Friday when Becky snagged me by the arm.

"Morgan," she gasped, short of breath. "I'm glad I ran into you."

"Why? What's the matter?"

"I've lost my wallet. It's got my student card in it, driver's license, and over twenty-five dollars."

"It's okay," I assured her. "We'll find it. Where did you have it last?"

"In my room, but maybe we should check the cafeteria." Her wide eyes relaxed as she smiled at two guys walking by.

"Well, did you look in your room?"

She turned and stared at me. "What?"

"I said—"

"Yeah, yeah." She threaded her arm through mine. "Let's go."

We hadn't gone ten feet, before Becky stopped to talk with a girl from one of her classes. I don't know how long we would've stood there, but unlike us, she apparently had someplace to go.

"Becky, you don't seem to be in any big rush to find your wallet. I'd be freaking out. You and Mimi are usually packed and ready to leave for the weekend by now. Does she know—" I stopped dead in my tracks, my heart also. "Wait a minute. What's going on? Is my mom here? Is that what this is all about?"

"No! Of course not." She did an about-face, taking me with her. "You know I'd come right out and tell you if that were true."

"Then what's going on?"

"Nothing. Here." She tossed me her purse, then leaned down, untied and retied the laces on both shoes. "But you know, now that I'm thinking about it, my wallet could be in the desk drawer."

"Are you okay? I've never seen you act so peculiar."

"Peculiar? What an ugly thing to say." She gave a half-hearted laugh. "And all this time I thought we were best friends."

"We are, but—"

"Come on." She took her purse from me and struck out, taking long steady strides. "I'll buy you a Coke when we get back."

"Becky?" I ran to catch up. "We're right here at the cafeteria. Don't you at least want to check?"

"No. I'm positive it's in my room. I don't know where my head is sometimes."

"Me either," I mumbled under my breath.

"I heard that."

When we made it back to the dorm, I intended to follow Becky to her room in hopes her wallet was there, but she had other plans.

"Let's go by your room first, so you can get rid of that armload of books."

"But your room is down the hall. Mine's on the third floor."

She shrugged. "That's okay. I don't mind."

"Becky..."

"Don't argue with me."

As we climbed the stairs, she rummaged her pockets and pulled out some change. "Sure hope I've got enough for our drinks."

"It doesn't matter. I'm not really thirsty."

"Well I am." She took off for the lounge once we reached the third floor. "Dump those books and come on."

By the time I tossed everything on the bed and grabbed some change off the nightstand, Becky had disappeared.

With every step, I grumbled about her bizarre behavior. Something was up, and I knew it. There were too many cars still in the parking lot for this place to be so quiet.

I jerked the door open.

"Surprise!"

Streamers and balloons hung from the ceiling. A semicircle of girls stood next to a table holding a luscious white cake with pink writing. My eyes watered as I read the icing print, Congratulations Morgan and Chuck.

Becky stepped beside me laughing, then leaned over and whispered. "Sorry for being so pee-cu-liar, Miss Smarty-Britches."

"I have to admit, I was really beginning to worry about you."

A familiar voice spoke behind me. "I hope you won't mind a bunkmate tonight."

"Janet!" I threw my arms around her neck. "I can't believe you're here." I reached for her hand and faced the rest of the girls. "I can't believe any of it. How'd y'all put this together so quick and without me finding out?"

Jennifer spoke up, "You were too busy to notice."

Wendy patted the couch. "Come over here and open your gifts while we cut the cake."

As soon as I sat, Ann picked up a gift and placed it in my lap. "Mine first."

While I peeled off the decorative blue and pink wrapping, snickering began. I lifted a flimsy white nightgown from its box. Someone whistled, followed by an outburst of laughter.

"You get to wear it, but it's really for Chuck," Mimi Clair clapped.

My face grew hot. "I don't know what to say."

Paula handed me the next gift. "And here's a little something to wear on your wedding day."

Again, warmth radiated up my neck. "Well, I'd like to think it would cover more than the last outfit, but I don't see how that's possible when the package fits in my hand."

The room erupted again with laughter.

"You'll find out. Open it," Paula insisted.

I removed a blue garter from the wrappings.

"Another gift for Chuck," Mimi sang out.

"Hold it up and look this way, Morgan." The flash on Becky's camera left spots dancing before my eyes.

Then she passed me a silver foil wrapped box. "It's nothing fancy."

I tore away the paper. "A mixer! Thanks, Becky."

"No more lumpy potatoes." She winked. A secret only she and I shared.

After I unwrapped a cookbook, an apron, and various kitchen gadgets, Janet reached over and presented me with a large white box. "I saved mine for last. It's from Mother and me. We hope you like it."

"From the cradle to the grave." Janet always said about our friendship.

I broke the taped edges, lifted the lid, and drew back the white tissue paper. "Oh, Janet." I ran my hand over the white, woven material.

"Hold it up. We want to see."

I stood and held a simple, but beautiful, white A-line dress.

"You always said it was important for you to wear white on your wedding day, remember? But you didn't want anything too frou-frou, so we decided on this style. Then we narrowed the material choices down to brocade, fancy cotton weave, or organza."

"Which one is this?"

"Brocade."

"It's perfect."

I hugged her tight. "Thank you. Thank you all."

Some of the girls began to gather bows and wrapping paper. Others talked and had second pieces of cake. I focused on the girls as a group, then individually. Two months ago I'd arrived at Midway with only one thought in mind—escape. I came here with a huge wall securely in place around me. A wall built for self-protection, which very few people penetrated. My self-worth had been shattered through years of name-calling and physical abuse. I'd become good at masking the pain and covering up the evil of others. What did these girls see in me? What did I have to offer in return? Why would they befriend someone so broken?

Panic gripped me. How would they respond when they discovered I'd lied to them?

Chapter 15

Janet and I stayed up most of the night laughing and talking and, with everyone gone for the weekend, slept in. Since the cafeteria had surely stopped serving breakfast, she and I decided to take a quick shower then check out Eddie's.

"Morgan, there's someone downstairs to see you." Janet's voice echoed through the large community bathroom.

After turning the water off, I removed the shower cap and ran my fingers through my hair. "How do you know?"

"Didn't you hear it? Somebody paged overhead. I'm almost dressed. You want me to go see who it is?"

"That's all right. I won't be but a minute."

"What if it's your mother?"

I clutched the towel to my chest. "She'd never have me paged. Besides, I can't imagine her taking off from work on a Saturday morning." Or would she?

"Maybe it's Chuck?"

"No. He's already left for work by now." I pushed my arms through the sleeves of a red, plaid shirtdress and buttoned the front. "I'll be right back."

A guy with broad shoulders and dark wavy hair stood when I

walked into the waiting area off the lobby.

I could have guessed all day but never in a month of Sundays would Richard Webster have come to mind. Mom had tried several times to get me to go out with him. "His family is well known and respected in the community," she would say. Maybe so, but Richard held no admiration in my eyes.

I held my head up and my back straight in an attempt to cover an uneasy feeling. "Hi. What brings you here?"

He smiled and looped a thumb in the front pocket of his Levi's. "Your mother. She told me you stayed on campus most weekends, and that I should come by sometimes. Dad had an excellent cotton crop this year, so I'm on my way to Memphis to pick out a new car." He winked. "I thought maybe you'd enjoy spending the day with yours truly."

I cringed at his presumptuous attitude, but also felt a twinge of pity. "I'm sorry you've gone out of your way. I wish you'd called first. Janet's here for the weekend, and we have plans."

"Janet Barnes?" His voice turned cool and crisp.

"That's right."

"Hmm." He ran well-manicured fingers through his hair. "Well, how about tomorrow night? I'm sure you must get bored here. Things look pretty dead. Why don't I drive up and take you for a spin? We could—"

"I don't think so. But thanks."

He stepped closer. "I'm not taking no for an answer. Your mother said to tell you, you've got her permission."

"No." I glared straight into his eyes.

"What's the matter, Morgan? Don't you think you'd have a good time?" His eyes shifted to other parts of my body.

Anger and humiliation radiated from my face.

Catching me off guard, he reached up and placed his hand

behind my neck then pulled me forward. He spoke into my ear. "Most girls jump at a chance to go out with me."

I knocked his hand away and stepped back. "Well, it's too bad I'm *not* 'most girls'. Good luck with your car shopping." I turned and walked away.

"Morgan, wait."

Everything inside me screamed, "Run!" But I kept a steady pace. I didn't relax until I reached the top of the stairs.

Janet glanced up from my music composition book when I rushed into the room. "That didn't take long."

"Longer than I wanted."

"What do you mean?"

I flopped onto the bed next to her. "Richard Webster was here. He asked me to go to Memphis with him."

She tossed the book to the side. "Yuck. Why?"

I took a deep breath and blew out the air slowly to calm my agitation. "It sounded like Mom encouraged him to come."

"Doesn't she know about his reputation with girls? I thought you told her?"

"I tried. Marsha tried. She doesn't believe it."

"Right. She can think the worst about her own children but not someone else's—" Janet reached for my hand. "I'm sorry. I shouldn't have said that."

I shook my head. "Not if their family has money. But hey, don't worry about it. Let's go get breakfast." I reached for a sweater in the closet, but instead pulled out the dress Janet and her mother made for me. "Just looking at this makes everything seem so real. It's going to happen." A tingling sensation ran up my spine. "Think about it…the next time we see each other, I'll be Mrs. Chuck Mathews."

"You mean, Mrs. Charles Jefferson Mathews."

"Hmm…you're right. I've never called him Charles before. It sounds so…strange."

"Morgan, you have a visitor in the lobby," Mrs. Henderson's voice rang out over the intercom.

Janet arched both eyebrows. "He won't take no for an answer, will he?"

"I don't know, but this time, we're both going." I nodded toward the door.

When Janet and I walked into the lobby, I exhaled upon seeing Kyle. But my diversion was short lived. His trademark smile was absent.

"What's wrong?" I asked, unsure I wanted to hear the answer. He didn't respond. "Kyle, you're scaring me." I searched his eyes, but he wouldn't hold my gaze. My heart pounded as if trying to force its way from my chest. "Is it Chuck?"

"Morgan, there's been an accident."

My lungs stopped working. The room began to spin. I reached to grab his arms but held only his shirt. "He's not…" My throat clogged and wouldn't allow me to complete the question.

He shook his head. "He's been taken to the Bradford County Hospital. From what the family has been told, a car pulled out in front of him outside Greer early this morning. Chuck left the road to avoid a head-on collision. The embankment was steep. The car rolled. It's totaled. They say the other driver had been drinking, but wasn't hurt."

"I've…I've got to get there. I've got to get to the hospital." I darted toward the doorway to the hall. "It won't take me long to pack a few things."

"You can stay at my house tonight." I heard Janet say, but her next words, "how bad is he," jarred my attention back to Kyle.

He looked at me. "I don't know. I haven't seen him. I came

straight here. But the family's concerned."

From the moment Kyle's news sank in, I began to pray for God's healing touch on Chuck. My stomach quivered like a school of fish swimming against the current. *God, please let him be okay.*

Within minutes, Janet and I had our bags packed and were back downstairs. For the first time since arriving at Midway, I signed out in the logbook indicating I was leaving the campus. Janet's and Kyle's cars waited in front of the dorm, loaded with our luggage.

"Why don't y'all follow me to the city limits of Greer, then Morgan can ride with me to the hospital," Kyle suggested.

"We're not stopping, Kyle. We'll follow you all the way in. I don't want to leave Morgan."

"We need to hurry. It's a two-and-a-half hour drive. The sooner we leave, the sooner we get there."

Every stoplight in town had it in for us. Every mile crawled by at an infant's pace, though the speedometer showed Janet driving well over the speed limit. We spoke very little, but I talked nonstop to God.

When I spotted the hospital, waves of nausea slammed into me, but by the time we parked and ran toward the front entrance, calm replaced it.

Kyle checked at the main desk. Chuck had been admitted to the third floor.

"That's a good sign, don't you think?" Janet spoke as we walked toward the elevator. "At least he's not in one of the units."

I didn't answer. All I wanted was to see him and know he was all right. When the doors opened and we walked toward the nurses' station, someone called Kyle by name. Chuck's brother, Marvin, walked in our direction.

"How is he?" Kyle and I asked simultaneously.

"He's in a lot of pain."

"At least he's awake." Janet remained positive.

"Can I see him, Marvin? Just for a moment?"

"Morgan, he's beat-up pretty badly. He's got stitches inside his mouth, on his face, and the top of his head… A cracked rib, a broken arm. The doctor's mostly concerned about his head."

"I've got to see him."

Chuck's brother gave Kyle a concerned look.

"She'll be okay, Marvin. I'll go with her."

"I'll wait here," Janet whispered.

Kyle and I followed Marvin down the hall and stopped outside what I assumed was Chuck's room. "Let me go in first and make sure he's presentable. Maybe I can talk Mother into going home or at least getting something to eat."

After the door closed behind Marvin, Kyle turned to me. "Morgan, if we get in there and it's too much for you, tug on my hand, and we'll leave, okay?"

I glanced at Kyle and nodded while biting the edge of my thumbnail.

The door opened. Mrs. Mathews passed me without acknowledging my presence, and then Marvin was there, motioning us to enter. I took a deep breath, forced a smile, and took Kyle's hand as we stepped inside. Even with everything Marvin had told us, I wasn't prepared for what I saw. A jolt of fear ran through my body. Kyle let go of my hand and gripped my shoulders. I reached for Chuck's hand.

I licked my lips and swallowed hard before attempting to speak. "Chuck, it's Morgan."

Chuck squeezed my hand before looking at me through squinted eyes. "How'd you know I was here?" He grimaced with every word.

"I told her," Kyle answered. "I didn't want her to hear about it over the phone or from somebody else."

Chuck peeked in Kyle's direction. "Nobody will tell me about the car. How bad is it?"

"Sorry, man. It's history. You won't be driving it again."

Chuck closed his eyes. A tear slipped from the corner of his eye, trailed down the line of his strong jaw to drip on the pillow. "I'm sorry, Morgan."

I swallowed past the lump in my throat. "Don't worry about anything but getting better," my voice quivered. I wanted to say more, but couldn't without bawling my head off.

"Excuse me, but I need to get his vitals," a clipped voice sounded from behind me. I turned my head and stared at the white uniform until I heard her next command, "If y'all don't mind waiting outside."

I leaned forward and whispered, "I'll be back in a minute, Chuck."

His eyes moved under their lids, but he didn't attempt to open them again. Instead, he squeezed my hand before releasing it.

Marvin led us to a nearby waiting room where Janet met me at the door. "How is he?"

"Oh, Janet, he looks awful, but I know it could have been worse."

"Yes, it could have been a lot worse." Chuck's mother sat rigid in a nearby chair. Her fingers gripped a Styrofoam cup. "He could have been killed." She directed an unwavering glare in my direction. "He's pushed himself too hard, Morgan. He's too young to think about marriage and take on all these changes and responsibility. Much less give up a job that pays the amount of money he makes. I've tried talking to him. Now it's time for you to tell him. If you love him and want what's best for him, you'll tell him." She stood and left the room. Marvin trailed behind her.

Janet stood beside me. "She's upset, Morgan. Don't let her get to you."

"It's too late. She already has."

Chapter 16

I sat on the edge of a Naugahyde chair watching over Chuck. His chest, unguarded in sleep, moved with a steady rhythm.

A nurse slipped in. "Visiting hours are over. Everyone but his immediate family will have to leave now." She checked his I.V., smoothed the covers, and finally left.

I glanced at Mrs. Mathews, hoping she would confirm I was family. She didn't. I don't know why I expected her to be any different. Her actions and earlier remarks made it clear she wasn't ready to accept me, any more than my parents would accept Chuck.

I shivered as we walked to Janet's car, grateful for Kyle's escort. The starless night closed around us, lending a gloom I couldn't shake. The damp chill added to a feeling of dread. Chuck lay battered, bruised, and in pain, yet I couldn't help or even comfort him. In fact, I'd only hurt him more by drawing him into my dysfunctional world.

Kyle promised to pick me up tomorrow morning then shut the passenger door. Janet slid into the driver's seat. She started the car, eased out of the hospital parking lot, and headed toward Greer.

Streetlights danced across the window. The coolness of the

leather bench matched the numbness within me.

Janet's voice washed over me before her words sank into my consciousness. "She's upset, Morgan. People say things they don't mean when they're under stress. Chuck would have a fit if he knew what his mother said to you."

I jerked my head toward her. "Don't you dare tell him."

"I won't, but you should."

"Maybe his mother's right. Sometimes I wonder if we'd be getting married so young if things were different with my parents."

Janet glanced at me and quickly turned her attention back to the road. "What are you saying? That you're marrying Chuck to get away from your parents?"

"You know that's not true." I shot back, angry she, of all people, would suggest such a thing.

"Then why are you talking this way?"

"Look, I'm ready to get married and for all the right reasons. But think about all the pressure Chuck must be under with the move and the new job. He has to make enough money for food, house, clothing, and doctor bills. I'm more of a burden to him than a help. Marriage is a huge responsibility."

"Are you just now thinking about all this? Because if you are—"

"No. Yes. Maybe I haven't looked at it hard enough from his perspective. I don't want him to wake up one day, regretting everything he had to give up."

Janet shook her head. "Boy, his mother sure did a number on you. This is so like you."

"What's that supposed to mean?"

"Why do you always doubt that people like you for you? Why can't you see that Chuck asked you to marry him because he loves you, and he's ready to get married?"

"I know he loves me. It's...oh, I don't know." I leaned my head back against the seat. "I'm too tired and upset to think straight. Can we talk about something else?"

"All right, but first, I want you to promise you won't do anything stupid. At least not until Chuck is better and the two of you talk this out. Promise me."

"Of course I'll talk to him. He needs to understand we don't have to get married right away. Especially now. His body needs time to heal. He has to replace his car, and who knows how all this might affect his new job. We may have to postpone the wedding for a while."

"And you're okay with that?"

I looked out the passenger window into darkness. "I'll have to be."

#

After a restless night, I woke to the murmur of voices coming from the kitchen, Janet and her mother. The smell of sizzling bacon wafted through the back bedroom. My stomach rumbled, reminding me how little I'd eaten in the past twenty-four hours. I took a quick shower and began dressing.

"You better hurry it up, Morgan." Mr. Barnes's gruff tone never could mask his kind heart. "We'll start without you if you're not at the table in two seconds."

In the kitchen, Janet's mother handed me a cup of steaming, hot chocolate. "We're sorry about Chuck's accident, but thankful he's okay. Janet wasn't sure how long he'd be in the hospital."

"I don't know either. Kyle and I are going back this morning to check on him."

"Well, sit down and let's bless the food so you can eat before he gets here."

Before I brought the first bite of egg to my mouth, the phone rang. My emotions churned. Was Kyle calling to report a change in Chuck's condition?

Mrs. Barnes answered, glanced in my direction, and cupped her hand over the mouthpiece. "Morgan, it's your mother."

My stomach clenched. I rose slowly, walked over, and reached for the phone with trembling hands. Before I could say more than hello, Mom's rant began. "You can't help yourself can you? You had to go running when you heard your precious Chuck had been in an accident. I understand alcohol was involved."

"The other driver had been drinking, Mom, not Chuck."

"That's not what I hear, but you always stick your head in the sand when it comes to that boy. I knew when I heard he was in the hospital you'd left Midway, and sure enough, Mrs. Henderson confirmed my suspicion. What time does Janet or her mother plan on bringing you home?"

"Kyle should be here any minute to—"

"I don't want that boy in my house. Do you hear me? He can let you out at the end of the driveway."

"He's taking me to the hospital to see Chuck."

"So you're not coming here? Had you planned to sneak into town then leave without saying a word? This is the thanks we get for sending you to college, doing without so you could have? You ungrateful…Wait until your father hears about this."

I wanted desperately to hang up, but I didn't have the guts.

Mom continued venting. "We've raised you to do better, but you've never been anything but a disappointment and an embarrassment. One of these days, when he gets through using you, maybe you'll wake up. Did you ever think this wreck was God's way of punishing you both? He's nothing but trash and—"

"Stop it! You have no right to say those things."

"Don't you talk to me in that tone. I have every *right*. I'm your mother."

"Why, Mom?" My chin quivered. "I wish I knew why."

"Why what? Why must I talk to you like you're a child? Because you are a child. Enjoy the rest of this semester, Morgan."

When Mom slammed the phone down, I wanted to run from the room, hide, and pretend the past twenty-four hours never happened, but I couldn't. Janet's family was waiting for me. But the ever-present tears lurked so close. Stinging. Burning. Deep breaths. I had to go back to the table even if I wouldn't be able to swallow a single bite.

"I'm sorry." Unable to make eye contact, I draped the napkin back in my lap and smoothed it over and over.

Janet's mother patted my arm. "Don't you worry about it."

Mr. Barnes's kiss on my cheek dislodged tears I quickly batted away.

Kyle's arrival allowed me to stop pushing the food around my plate. I gathered my belongings and thanked Janet and her family for their help and then hugged them good-bye.

#

When Kyle and I arrived on the third floor of the hospital, I was relieved to see Chuck's father open the door to Chuck's room. Even more relieved when I found out his mother had stayed home.

His father took my hand and led me to Chuck's bedside. "This is all the medicine you need right here, son."

If possible, Chuck's bruised and swollen face appeared more painful than it had last night, yet the doctor had already written his discharge order. Chuck lay on top of the bedcovers in pajamas, robe, and house shoes, waiting for the nurses to complete the appropriate paperwork. He winced when he reached for my hand.

"Are you sure you're not leaving too soon?" I kissed his cheek, avoiding his swollen lips.

"I'm sure. I've got too much to do, and *you*," he squeezed my hand and took a shallow breath, "need to get back to Midway before your parent's find out you left."

I didn't dare tell him it was too late. He had enough to worry about.

He peered past me to his friend. "Kyle will drive you back. Won't you?"

Kyle nodded. "Already been discussed and decided."

The nurses interrupted us with paperwork and instructions. Chuck moved slowly, refusing help, although at times he couldn't avoid a moan of pain. Once he was seated in the wheelchair, I walked beside him and held his hand until we reached the front curve where his father waited. I let go and stood back while Kyle helped him into the cab of the truck. Chuck held his side and grimaced as he eased back against the seat. I leaned in and kissed him good-bye on the cheek.

"I'll see you in a few days," he spoke through clenched teeth.

I swallowed hard and nodded. Kyle dropped an arm around my shoulders as Chuck's dad drove away. "He's going to be fine, Morgan."

#

Midway held mixed emotions for me. I had no choice but to return. After all, we weren't married. It wouldn't be proper—even if it were possible—for me to stay and take care of him. My heart ached. Even Kyle's promise to keep an eye on Chuck didn't comfort me.

By midafternoon, I couldn't stand it any longer. I gathered all my change, walked to the phone room, and dialed Chuck's grandmother. He had moved in with her after his grandfather's death three years ago. He didn't have to go far; she lived next door to his parents on a small plot of country ground. I was sure Chuck would be recovering in his own bed.

A sweet, but strong voice answered, "Hello."

"Mrs. Cox, it's Morgan. I wondered if I could talk with Chuck?"

"Who'd you say?"

"Morgan. Morgan Selby."

"Yes, Morgan. Honey, Chuck's not here. He's staying at his mother's for a few days. I guess you heard about his wreck."

"That's why I'm call—"

"They say he's lucky to be alive. I don't know what we would've done if we'd lost him. The Lord was sure looking after him."

Chuck's grandmother continued without missing a beat, rambling praises and concerns, which I silently agreed with wholeheartedly. I studied the coins in my hand. "Mrs. Cox, I don't have a lot of money—"

"Oh, honey, I'm so sorry."

"No, I mean, I'm using a payphone, and I don't have a lot of change. I need to hang up and try to get in touch with Chuck."

"Well, he's at his mother's. Do you have the number?"

"Yes, ma'am."

I thanked her, hung up, dialed the Mathews's residence, and fed more money into the phone base. I cringed when Mrs. Mathews answered with an agitated tone. Her mood didn't improve when I announced myself and asked to speak with Chuck.

"He's resting right now, and I don't think we should bother him. It's been a rough day for him, for all of us. He needs his rest. I'll let him know you called, Morgan."

I plodded back to my room, thinking about all the different

people and circumstances that had tried to stand between Chuck and me, yet our love for each other remained strong. Once again, I had no choice but to wait and pray. I reached for my Bible and turned to the marker in Psalms. A group of words jumped off the page. *In God have I put my trust: I will not be afraid what man can do unto me.*

I pondered the words: God, trust, fear, man. A shiver ran through my body. I felt a strong urgency to decide which one would rule my life, fear of man or trust in God?

God, you're right. I believe in You, but I haven't been trusting in You. Not really. It's hard for me. I haven't had good experience with trust. I'm afraid, but I'm tired of living in fear. Today, I put my trust in You, my true Father, my protector. Help me to hold on to Your hand and to face whatever comes my way in this life.

Meg, a brunette from down the hall, opened the door. "Morgan, you have a phone call."

Chapter 17

Once again mixed emotions assailed me as I moved toward the phone room. I hoped it was Chuck calling, but Mom could also be waiting on the other end of the line. With each step, I asked God for courage then took a deep breath as I reached for the dangling receiver.

"Hello?"

"Morgan," my sister greeted. "It's Marsha."

"Hey." I laughed and plopped into a nearby chair. "What a nice surprise. I thought it might be Mom."

"And you came to the phone? Why?"

Seconds passed. "I guess...because she's our mom."

"Some things never change. You think being our mom gives her the right to treat us like a dog, and you're obligated to take it? The answer, dear sister, is no. Keep that in mind next time she calls, which I'm guessing could be tonight."

A shiver ran through me. "Why do you say that?"

"I just got off the phone with her. I threatened to hang up if she didn't stop screaming. She's on a tear about you being in Greer and not coming by the house. You know the always present 'what will the neighbor's think'? Well, that's the only reason you're still at Midway. She's afraid to pull you out before the semester's over. People may think you flunked out. Or worse, you're pregnant."

I gripped the phone tighter and sprang to my feet. "She said that? She said people might think I'm pregnant?" The words spewed out in anger.

"Yep. You know how she is. Don't let it get to you. But if I were you, I'd keep a low profile for a while. Stay out of Greer. She's not likely to forget what you've done anytime soon. How's Chuck doing by the way?"

My stomach quivered at the thought of the amount of pain he must be in. "He looks awful. But his worst injuries are a broken arm and cracked ribs. He's at his mom's. We haven't had a chance to really talk about how all this will affect him—us, but it'll cause some major changes."

"What do you mean?"

Marsha was the one person—other than Chuck—whom I'd always trusted. "Chuck asked me to marry him."

"Congratulations!" Marsha squealed two octaves higher than usual.

"Yeah, we found out we could get married in Alabama as soon as I turn eighteen. We had..." I blew out a breath of disappointment. "We had the date planned and everything."

"Had? So, what's the problem?"

"Don't you see? The accident changes everything. I don't have a clue how long it takes for cracked ribs and a broken arm to heal, but it'll take more than a week. And by then, he's supposed to be starting a new job here. Since Mr. Fisher's already accepted his two weeks' notice, Chuck could end up without a job altogether. And his mother...Ugh! She won't even let me talk to him on the phone."

"Chuck can handle his mother. Don't let her keep you away

from him, Morgan. And I'd think after all the years he's worked for Mr. Fisher, the old coot would probably be more than happy to keep him employed. Broken bones or not."

"True, but I feel so guilty. All the expenses Chuck never would've had if it wasn't for me. A six-month lease for a house here that'll have to be paid even if he stays in Greer. I've got to do something to help. Even if it means dropping out of Midway to get a job."

"Are you crazy? And live where? Mom and Dad would drag your behind back home so fast. Don't be stupid, Morgan. Promise me you'll stay in college."

"I'll stay for now, but I *am* getting a job."

"You'd better work on keeping your grades up. Are you passing everything?"

"I won't make the Dean's list, but surprisingly, I'm doing really well."

"Then why not stay in school and get an education?" Marsha's big sister's voice of authority demanded.

"Majoring in music was Mom's idea," I responded in a huff, "not mine."

"So change your major. People do it all the time. And, Morgan, make sure you're marrying Chuck for the right reason. Don't make the same mistake I did when I married Bob...just to get out of their house. Married life may not be all you've hoped for."

"There's a big difference between us, Marsha. I love Chuck."

"Then I hope it works out. But remember, Mom's threatening to pull you out of college in January. You'll be eighteen before then, maybe married, but regardless, neither she nor Dad can legally force you to do anything. Meanwhile, don't give Dad a reason to get his hands on you again."

I shuddered. "I don't plan on it."

"Well, after hearing from Mom, I thought I'd better check on you. Take care."

#

The next morning, I woke with a mission—find a job. After my last class, I put in an application at Eddie's, at a nearby dime store, and two dress shops. Later that night, I sat in my room and scanned the Help Wanted page of the local newspaper. Most of the jobs were full-time positions. Much of what remained didn't look promising.

Ann stuck her head in the door. "Chuck's on the phone."

I tossed paper in the air and bolted down the hall.

"Hello!" I panted, trying to catch my breath.

"Hey. Somebody chasing you?"

A big grin stretched my face. It was good to hear his voice. "Chuck," I breathed his name, loving the feel of it on my lips. "I hoped you'd call tonight. How do you feel?"

"Like I've been in a car wreck."

I chuckled at his attempt to be his old self. "You must be feeling a little better. You weren't making wisecracks in the hospital."

"It's hard to joke when you're lying on a lumpy, plastic mattress while your ribs are screaming with each breath. I'll make it though. The pain can't last forever."

"I miss you."

"I miss you, too, Blue Eyes. I'll see you soon. Do you need anything?"

"Yeah, for you to get better. I love you."

"Love you, too. I'll call you tomorrow night."

Chuck put up a good front, but he sounded weak and frequently stopped between words to take a shallow breath. I reminded myself that each day would bring him improvement and less pain.

And who knows, maybe tomorrow I'd find that perfect job.

#

Wednesday afternoon, I got my first break. Al's Drug Store was hiring, and I sat waiting to talk to Al himself.

After thirty minutes, the number of people needing prescriptions filled dwindled. A short, stocky man in a white lab coat stepped from behind the pharmacy counter.

He walked up holding two white mugs with the smell of coffee wafting from them. "Hi, Morgan. I'm Allan Perkins." He nodded toward the woman behind the counter I'd given my application to. "Betty tells me you're going to Midway." He handed me a cup. "You don't look old enough to be going to college."

"I'll be eighteen next month." To be polite, I took a sip of the nasty stuff.

"I'm looking for someone who can give me a few hours a day during the week—and all day on Saturdays. You'd be expected to tidy up the shelves, send out monthly bills, and keep the ledgers straight. Have you ever used a ten-key adding machine?"

"Yes, sir." I didn't lie. Janet and I had played with her dad's a few times. We would time ourselves to see who could add the fastest without making any mistakes.

"The job pays a buck-fifteen an hour."

"Sounds great."

He took a few leisurely sips from his mug while he studied my face.

I squirmed worse than a two-year-old in Church on a hot August Sunday. *Say it. Please say it.* What could be taking him so long? He needed help, and I needed a job.

"I can start anytime."

Al stood. "I better get back to work." He drained his mug then nodded toward the front counter again. "Talk to Betty. You two work out some kind of schedule, but I'll need you here this Saturday."

Twenty-three hours a week. I'd have to work hard to prove myself, but math had been one of the few subjects where I excelled. I envisioned an adding machine and mentally moved my fingers to each invisible number. By Saturday, I was sure I'd look like I knew what I was doing.

A damp, dusty scent permeated the air. Wind blew my hair in every direction. Wrapped up in my success, I'd failed to notice the swirling clouds now obscuring the sun. I held my dress down to keep it from blowing up and sprinted the two blocks to the dorm. In my excitement, I could've run two more. I couldn't wait to tell Chuck my news, but I wanted to tell him in person and see his surprised expression.

#

Saturday morning I woke as thunder shook the building.

"Not again." I opened the curtains and gazed out at a torrential Mississippi downpour. The rain fell in sheets so thick I couldn't see sky or ground. Without a raincoat or car, I had visions of a drenched dog. Then I remembered a plastic rain bonnet my grandmother had given me. I'd never worn the thing and promised myself I never would. But today, I'd humbly eat my words. After emptying my purse onto the bed, my fingers explored an inside pocket and retrieved the priceless item.

By ten after seven, I stood at the front door of the dorm tying the straps of the accordion creased, rain hat under my chin. The thing swallowed my head. After making sure no one was watching,

I took the garbage bags I'd removed from the wastebasket and slipped them over each foot, shoe and all. Then used rubber bands to secure them.

With all the wind, my umbrella proved useless, and despite my efforts, I arrived at the drugstore with soaked feet.

Betty greeted me with a pleasant smile. "I hope it doesn't keep this up all day. You can put your wet things back here." She walked toward the backroom. "And then I'll show you around."

She never said a word about my plastic attire.

The tour took only minutes. Cleaning supplies were stored in the bathroom. A desk stood in the far corner of the musty oversized closet where I'd hung my coat and stashed my wet items. Boxes stacked halfway to the ceiling and covered all but a narrow path from the door to the desk. "This is the stockroom as well as your office. I hope you're not claustrophobic," she teased and opened the top desk drawer. "Here's the ledger. When you're not working on the books, you'll clean and stock the shelves. If you have any questions, let me know."

The hardest part of the bookkeeping task was trying to read Betty's handwriting. Her letters and numbers slanted so badly, they were almost flat. I found if I turned the book to the left at an angle, her writing became almost readable.

Around noon, Mr. Perkins entered my closet-office. "I'm ordering hamburgers, what do you want on yours?"

I shook my head. "I'm not really hungry." I'd enjoyed the work so much, I hadn't thought about food. "Thank you though."

"Nonsense, you've got to eat, and I'm buying. I don't expect you to go out in this mess." He raised his arm toward a windowless wall. "It'll be easier on both of us if you tell me what you want."

Something about his gray-blue eyes, framed by laugh-lines, calmed my spirit. "Okay. Make mine with everything but onions."

He reached in his pocket and laid a nickel and a dime on my desk. "Buy yourself something to drink from the machine."

"Thanks, Mr. Perkins, but you don't have to—" He'd left.

#

By midafternoon, I finished dusting the third aisle of metal racks and wiping all the merchandise with a damp cloth. I started down the stepladder, when someone put a hand on my waist. Startled, I spun around and smacked into the person's head with my elbow.

"Chuck! You scared me half to death. Did I hurt you?"

He sucked in a breath through clenched teeth and held the side of his face. "I'm okay. It's my fault. I didn't mean to frighten you."

I hopped off the ladder and pulled his hand away. Shades of yellows and greens resided where black and blue bruises had been a week ago. Puckered pink skin surrounded the stitches, but his lips were no longer swollen. His left arm rested in a sling. "I'm so sorry." I wanted so badly to throw my arms around him and kiss him silly.

Chuck caught my hand with his good one. "I went by the dorm. Mrs. Henderson told me where to find you. What's going on?"

I stood taller. "I got a job. Today's my first day. I would've told you, but I wanted it to be a surprise."

He didn't smile. "Well, I'm surprised. Kyle and his date, Patty, are waiting in the car out front. It's rained so much this week he couldn't get in the fields, and I wanted to see you...what time do you get off?"

"Six." I searched his eyes to catch a hint of his mood. Could he be angry? Maybe the blow to his head caused more pain than he was letting on.

"We'll be back to get you then. I wish you'd discussed it with me first."

We stared at each other in silence.

"We'll talk tonight." He leaned down and kissed my forehead before walking away.

This was not the reaction I envisioned. All the excitement and pride of my newfound job disappeared like air from a pinpricked balloon.

Chapter 18

Not a single star shone. A fine mist of rain continued to fall. The dreary night did nothing to dispel my disappointment over Chuck's reaction to my new job.

Kyle's car lights flashed across the house as he and his date backed out of the driveway, leaving Chuck and me standing on the front porch. Chuck fumbled with his keys, unlocked the door, and then stepped aside for me to enter. My nervous stomach quivered. A feeling I'd never experienced with him.

"Are you hungry? I had Patty pick up a couple of frozen pot pies at the grocery earlier."

"No." I dropped my purse on a nearby chair. "I've kinda lost my appetite." The words came out crisp and cold. We needed to talk, but I dreaded where this conversation might take us. We'd never had a serious argument. Never even came close. But tonight, for the first time in our relationship, Chuck had hurt and embarrassed me.

When Kyle and Patty rushed off to the movies, I was sure they'd been asked to give us time to work out our differences. My face burned hot thinking about Chuck sharing his disappointment in me. Maybe I should have discussed my job with him, but that was no excuse.

"I've missed you." He walked over and gently touched my face, then bent and pressed his lips to mine.

My emotions were being pulled like taffy. I loved Chuck more than words could describe. He'd never been anything but respectful, loving, and understanding, but could he have a darker side I'd yet to see?

"You look tired." He brushed strands of hair from my forehead. "Why don't you rest before we worry about supper?" He laced his fingers with mine and led me to the sofa.

Someone once told me that making up after a fight was nice. From my experience, I saw no truth in that statement. How could there be any sense of enjoyment after hurting someone you love? *God,* please *help me control my tongue.*

Chuck grimaced as he lowered himself to the sofa.

"You're still in a lot of pain, aren't you?"

"Yeah, but I'm getting there."

"What did the doctor say?"

He shrugged. "I'll find out Monday. He's supposed to remove the stitches then. I'll sure be glad. They're about to itch me to death. Now this thing," he moved his casted arm, "is what I'm really ready to part company with. I'm tired of lugging it around, but the doc's already said it'll take five to six weeks for the fracture to heal."

I rubbed my fingertips across the rough, white plaster. "Does your arm hurt much?"

He shook his head. "Not like the ribs."

"I'm glad you're doing better. It's been a long miserable week." I meant it. I'd grown accustomed to seeing him daily before his accident. We talked on the phone every evening while he recuperated at his mother's, but it wasn't the same as seeing with your eyes what words didn't always tell you.

He lifted my chin and brushed my lips with his. "It's been hard for both of us."

I rested my head against his shoulder and waited for the conversation to shift. I didn't have to wait long.

He kissed the top of my head. "Morgan, why didn't you tell me about the job?"

I sat up and faced him. "Can I ask you a question first?"

"Sure." He nodded.

Stay calm. "Why did you tell Kyle and Patty about being upset with me?"

"What?" He blinked and leaned forward, his hand resting on my knee. "I'm not upset with you."

"Then why did they make the flimsy excuse about going to the movies? You told me yourself that it would give us a chance to talk. You already made it clear earlier today that you weren't happy about my job. I believe you said, 'We'll talk about it tonight.' You want to talk, we'll talk, but I'm not going to be scolded like a child or talked down to. I've had enough of that to last me a lifetime. I know what the Bible says about the husband being head of the home. I believe it, but I won't ever allow anyone to mistreat me again. Verbally or physically."

Chuck's eyes widened. "Whoa! Where's this coming from?" He took a deep breath. "First of all, I would *never* deliberately hurt you. Second Kyle and Patty discussed on the way up here about going to the movies. I'm sure they wanted to give us some time alone. We haven't seen each other for a week." He studied my face. "Is that why you've been so quiet? You thought I'd discussed you and your job with the two of them?"

"Well didn't you?"

"No." He reached for my hand. "Morgan, I feel like I've been tried and convicted. Not because of what I did, but because of your parents. I'm not the enemy. I'll never belittle you. I'll never hit you or try to control you."

"Then why are you upset, disappointed, or whatever you want to call it, about me getting a job?"

"After we're married, if you want to work, I'm okay with that. Right now, you've got enough with school, your job at the dorm, and us getting married. I think it's too much."

More frustrated than angry, I jerked my hand from his. "You see?"

Chuck sighed. "Okay, let's go about this in a different way. Why don't you tell me why you wanted a job?"

How could I forget his mother's words, "He's too young to think about marriage and take on all these changes and responsibilities?"

"After everything that's happened—the wreck and all—you've got expenses you hadn't counted on. I wanted to help, and the only way I knew how was to get a job."

He smiled and recaptured my hand. "And I love you for it. But my insurance will pay for replacing the car. The hospital bill's covered. There *are no* extra expenses."

"What about your job?"

"What about it?"

I tugged on the sling cradling his arm. "I don't know a lot about cracked ribs, but I know you won't be lifting anything heavy for a while. And you've already said Mr. Edward wasn't happy when he heard you couldn't start work Monday. What makes you think he'll wait for your bones to heal? For all we know, he may have hired someone else by now."

"That's why I'm here. I talked to Mr. Edwards this afternoon. He has a nephew who wants to learn the trade. He's willing to give me another week to recover. He's even willing to hire his nephew to do all the lifting, but only if I train him. I told him I'd be there a week from Monday."

"What happens then? You'll train yourself right out of a job."

Chuck's eyes sparkled. "You do love to borrow trouble, don't you, Morgan Selby? I'm not worried about it." His smile vanished. "But we've jumped track. We need to talk about your job and us." He dipped his chin and peered directly into my eyes. "Do you know I love you?"

"Yes."

"Before today, have you ever felt I was trying to control you?"

"No."

He put his hand behind my neck and pulled my head to his shoulder. "I'm sorry for whatever I did that made you uncomfortable, but I'm glad you told me. We can't work things out if we don't talk about 'em."

We sat in silence, relief washing over me. "I'm sorry I didn't tell you first."

"We're okay, Morgan. Fill me in on this job of yours."

I jolted upright, grinning to share my day. "I love it. The people. The hours." I giggled, wondering what he'd think about my closet/office. "The pay. It's more than cleaning shelves, which is what you saw me doing. Mr. Perkins, my boss, hired me mainly to do light bookkeeping. A skill. A chance to gain experience that means something."

Chuck tipped my face toward his. "What did Mr. Perkins say when you told him you'd need some time off next month to get married?"

I bit my lip. "I didn't tell him."

Chuck's eyebrows pinched together. "Why not?"

"Because I didn't think we'd still be getting married next

month." My gaze shifted to my hands resting in my lap. "I figured it would take time to sort things out, and I didn't want you to feel like, because we set the date, we had to get married."

"Morgan, nothing's changed. We're getting married next month...Unless you're having second thoughts."

"Are you kidding? No."

"Then you've got to tell him. And don't be surprised if he gets upset."

"Maybe it'll help when I tell him I'll be available to work extra hours starting January... if that's all right with you?"

Chuck stood. "I know you've got to be hungry. I'm starving. Why don't you see what kind of meat pies Patty bought and turn the oven on. I'll be in there in a minute to help."

"But we haven't finished discussing my job."

"We can continue our talk in the kitchen. I'll be back." He walked down the hallway.

A little disappointed, I went into the kitchen, removed a metal ice tray and tonight's supper from the refrigerator freezer. The instructions on the boxes indicated the pies should be cooked at 375 degrees. With the stove set, I got on my knees and rambled through the cabinets to find a baking sheet.

Chuck caught me off guard as I stood at the sink washing my hands. He kissed the back of my neck, sending shivers up and down my spine.

"You scared me. I didn't hear you come in."

He stuck a small piece of paper under my nose, too close for me to read.

"What does it say?"

He drew away and waited for me to finish drying my hands before handing it to me.

"Five-hundred dollars? Chuck, why did you write me a check

for five-hundred dollars?"

"I want you to find a bank and open us an account. You'll need someplace to deposit your payroll check." He braced his hip against the counter. "If you still have a job after Monday."

"I don't need that much money."

"You'll be opening *us* an account. It's no longer about you or me; it's about the two of us. I don't believe in married couples having two accounts, his and hers. I don't think it's healthy. When I come back Monday, I'll bring the paperwork for you to sign on the accounts at the Bank of Greer. When we get married, we become one in every aspect. You've made it clear why you took the job at the drug store, and I'm okay with it. But in the future, we'll make all our decisions together. We'll talk it out. Okay?"

"Okay." I threw my arms around his neck. "No more surprises."

"Well, now I didn't say that. Sometimes surprises are a good thing."

I stepped back to better see him. "What's that supposed to mean?"

"Somebody I know has a birthday in a few days, and I may have a surprise or two up my sleeve."

"What?" I demanded.

He rubbed his nose against mine. "Now you know I can't tell you; you'll just have to wait."

Chapter 19

As Mr. Franklin's voice began to fade, my eyelids drooped. I fought to stay awake during his music composition lecture, but the stuffy room, combined with a lack of sleep, caused me to give in to my body's beckoning. Then chairs scraping across the floor jarred me awake. I wiped moisture from a corner of my mouth. My face burned hot at the instructor's disapproving glare. I picked up my books and trailed behind several students, hoping he wouldn't say anything.

Outside, the morning cold had given way to a November Indian summer. White, purple, and red chrysanthemums, along with a colorful starburst of dahlias, dotted the grounds. If not for the bare trees and the musty scent of decaying leaves, it would be easy to forget winter's approach.

"Hey, Morgan, you headed to the cafeteria?"

"I can't today, Sarah. I'll catch up with you tomorrow."

Lunch would be a Coke and a candy bar at best. I needed a thirty-minute nap. Thoughts of my feather pillow quickened my pace. I counted my steps back to the dorm, up the stairs, and into my room...and then stopped dead still. A brown, paper-wrapped package lay on the middle of my bed. I easily recognized the penmanship—Mom's.

I wanted to toss it aside. Just seeing her handwriting made me cringe. Instead, I plopped down, tore the wrapping from the box, and lifted the lid. A beautiful royal blue dress with a white collar nestled beneath layers of tissue paper. Light caught the elegant embroidered print edging the white cuffs. Nothing near as nice hung in my closet. My hands trembled as I reached for the sealed envelope that had fallen to the floor. I quoted my version of the verse hanging on the mirror, "I trust You, God, and I will no longer fear what man can do to me." In spite of my words, my hands continued to shake. The tremors had become a part of me, as though my body had been mis-wired. I opened the envelope and unfolded the letter.

Morgan,

Long before your father told you to get out of this house, you made your feelings perfectly clear. You never once came home for a visit. We felt that by closing the door to you, you would come to your senses. I've decided you don't have any. We've allowed you to get away with too much, and your behavior is now out of control and unacceptable. From now on, you will do as you are told, starting by coming home during Thanksgiving break. You will spend the entire time here. You might as well know you'll not be returning to Midway next semester. You will get a job and live here. If someday you prove yourself worthy, we'll talk about college then. We'll discuss this and more when you get home.

I've asked Richard Webster and he has graciously agreed to pick you up from school on the 27th. He's going out of his way to be courteous, and I expect the same from you.

I've noticed many girls wearing dresses so short

it leaves little to the imagination. I have no reason to doubt that, without my supervision, you've jacked every hemline up to whatever the school will allow. I've sent this dress, and I expect to see you in it without the hem altered. We will not tolerate you tramping around with your behind hung out while you're at home. You'll not embarrass this family further.

Happy Birthday,
Mother

I wadded the letter and threw it against the wall. Waves of nausea hit. I raced to the garbage can and vomited. Hot, angry tears dripped from my chin along with this morning's breakfast.

Long after the tears dried, anger remained. I cleaned the soiled wastebasket, washed my face and hands, and brushed my teeth. Then shoved the dress back into the box, stormed down the hall, and deposited it on Ann's bed. A gift given without love was *not* worth keeping. Using pen and paper from her desk, I placed a brief note on top of the box.

To Ann,

Enjoy!

She and I were the same size, and I knew she would indeed enjoy having a new dress.

#

I rolled over and looked at the clock, 2:07 a.m. "Happy eighteenth birthday," I whispered. I'd made it. With the covers tightly gathered around me, I allowed myself to drift back into the comfort of sleep.

#

I glanced at Chuck with a smile that stretched so wide my cheeks were beginning to hurt. "You still haven't told me where we're going."

"You'll see." A twinkle of mischief appeared in his eye. "We're almost there."

Chuck drove his new candy-apple red Mercury Cougar so slowly, I didn't think we'd ever get anywhere. But then I saw it: Bella's. The restaurant with all the charm of years gone by, the place where he'd asked me to marry him. "Oh, Chuck. I love this place."

"I thought you might." He turned into the parking lot and shut off the motor, before lifting my chin toward his. "Happy birthday, Morgan."

Chuck pressed his lips against mine then sighed as he pulled back and gazed into my eyes. "You ready to celebrate?"

I snuggled close, savoring the moment. "With you? Anytime."

Everything was the way I'd remembered. Irish linen tablecloths and napkins. Beautiful china and crystal. Warm candlelight and rock fireplace. The crackle of wood burning. Flames licked at the logs and cast dancing shadows around the dimly lit room. An ambience of romance. What a wonderful birthday.

The air carried the aroma of fresh bread, garlic, baked fish, and clam chowder—my favorites. My stomach rumbled.

The hostess led us to a secluded corner table and handed us menus. The waiter soon arrived and took our orders. Afterward, Chuck reached across the table and rubbed the top of my left hand. "I have a surprise for you."

I scanned the room then focused on him. "I thought *this* was my surprise."

"It's one of your surprises. I've contacted a pastor in Vernon, Alabama. We had a nice talk, and he's agreed to marry us."

I sucked in a huge breath. "How did you manage that?"

"Marybeth, my sister. The one who works at the courthouse, contacted someone in Vernon. She got the name and phone numbers of Baptist pastors in the area. Anyway, after talking to a couple of them, I made the arrangements. We're getting married as planned, the Tuesday before Thanksgiving."

My insides tingled. "What time?"

"One o'clock. I figured if we left here around seven we could drive to Danville to pick up my father and still have plenty of time to make it by then."

My stomach quivered. "You're sure your dad won't say anything?"

"I'm sure."

The waiter brought our salads and poured iced tea. Chuck thanked him and waited until he walked away. Then he reached across the table for my hands so we could bless the meal. An object pressed between our hands. My fingers itched to explore the strange item, but Chuck tightened his hold. I raised my head and peeked at him, but with his head bowed, he'd already begun the prayer. "Lord, thank You for this day, a special day for both of us. Be with us as we plan our journey in this life together. May our love continue to grow strong, and may our faith never waver. Direct our paths and protect us. Thank You for this meal, may it nourish our bodies. Amen."

At the end of the prayer, he gave my hand an extra little squeeze before removing his from mine. I stared at the item that remained. A ring. "What in the world?" I picked it up for a closer inspection then raised my eyes to meet his, too dumfounded to speak.

He grinned. "I've had it for weeks." Chuck placed the ring on my finger. "Aren't you going to say something? Do you like it?"

I gasped and nodded. "Yes…It's beautiful." I tipped my finger. Six brilliant-cut round diamonds surrounded a larger princess diamond. All sparkled reds and blues in the candlelight. Tears blurred my vision, casting an aura over the stones. My chin quivered. "It's perfect."

We leaned across the table. Our lips almost touched.

"Excuse me." The waiter cleared his throat. "Is everything all right, sir?"

We both laughed before Chuck answered, "Everything's fine."

During the slow drive back to the dorm, I rested my head against Chuck's shoulder. "I'll remember this night for the rest of my life."

"I know there have been times when neither of us thought this day would get here. And it's not been easy. Especially for you." He kissed the top of my head. "But we have a new life ahead of us now. Things are going to be better."

I didn't want to spoil the moment, but now was not the time to let our guard down. I knew my parents better than he did. I'd have to tell him about my mom's letter, but not tonight.

"You're too quiet, Morgan. What's wrong? What are you thinking?"

"We've still got two more weeks."

"Your parents can't stop us from getting married, and after we're married, they'll accept our marriage. You'll see. They'll have to."

You don't know them.

Chapter 20

"Look what I have," I sang as I strolled into Jennifer's room, gripping a box with both hands.

Wendy hopped from the edge of the desk and trotted over. "I hope it's something to eat. I'm starved."

"Well you're in luck. It's chocolate on chocolate."

"Chuck got you a cake?" Ann squealed.

"He sure did." I wanted to scream "that's not all!", but I decided to see how long it would take one of them to notice my beautiful engagement ring.

"What are we waiting for?" Wendy took the box and placed it on Jennifer's desk. She folded back the tabs and lifted the lid. A big gob of icing perched on top of her finger for a split second before she popped it in her mouth. "Mmm. Yep, it's chocolate."

Jennifer pushed herself off her bed. "Oh, for pity sakes, somebody sit on her while I go get some paper plates and utensils from the lounge."

"Morgan, we don't want to eat up your cake," Becky said.

"If she didn't want us to eat it, she wouldn't have brought it in. Right, Morgan?"

Before I could answer Wendy, Mimi Clair yanked my hand up.

"Where did you get that?"

Eyes turned from finger-dipping Wendy to Mimi and me. The room grew quiet. A slight twitch tugged one corner of my mouth before I squealed.

Mimi yanked my hand around to show everyone, snatching so hard I stumbled forward from the force. "Would you look at this!"

The girls closed in around, buzzing excitedly. My face hurt from smiling and laughing as they took turns admiring the ring.

"It's gorgeous. Look how it sparkles in the light," Paula said.

"Okay, you vultures, here's everything we need to devour—what are ya'll doing?" Jennifer's voice rose above the clamor.

"We've forgotten about the cake." Paula motioned Jennifer over. "You've got to come see this."

"I haven't forgotten about anything," Wendy shouted. "Give me that knife." She removed the harmless, plastic device from Jennifer's hand.

I shared the night's events as Wendy and Jennifer cut the cake and passed slices around.

Wendy stopped licking her fingers long enough to say, "Just think, in less than forty-eight hours, you'll be a married woman."

My smile faded. I took a deep breath and hoped they'd understand. "Not really."

"Um..." Paula swallowed. "What do you mean?"

I settled onto the foot of Jennifer's bed. "I'm not getting married this Friday. We've changed the date."

"Why?" Several of them chimed in unison.

"Remember me telling you about the phone call from Janet and her mother?"

Heads nodded. Others answered yes.

"Chuck and I didn't want to risk having our wedding plans spoiled or our marriage annulled. So, if my parents or someone *is* watching us closely, we've decided to wait them out."

"For how long?" Mimi Clair spoke around a mouthful of cake.

It was a legitimate question, but why did Mimi have to be the one asking? I pushed my scowl upward. "We've set a new date, but I don't want to say anything about that right now." I scanned a hodgepodge of expressions. Some stared at their plates and pushed crumbs of cake around. Others stared at me with their head cocked, wide eyed, or an eyebrow raised. "If Mom asks questions, I don't want any of y'all lying for me. She's also been known to call Mrs. Henderson. I don't think our dorm mother would, but if she does ask, it's best you tell her the truth: you don't know."

"You're not going to tell us, are you?" Mimi planted her hands on her hips.

I whirled toward her, anger rising to the surface. "No." It was beginning to look like my suspicions about her were dead on. "Not right now."

"Do you really think your parents would stop you from getting married if they knew how much y'all love one another?" Ann stood and gathered the plates. "I mean, it doesn't make sense. They can't stand guard over you for the rest of your life."

Knots twisted my stomach. "I have no doubt. They'll do whatever they feel necessary to keep me from marrying Chuck."

"Can't you even give us a hint of when or where you'll be getting married?" Mimi Clair whined.

I swallowed hard, trying to keep a lid on my anger. Her persistence seemed more than normal curiosity, even for her. But I didn't want anything or anybody spoiling this night.

Jennifer interrupted, "She said she didn't want to take any chances, so give it up, Mimi. Enough with the questions."

"Thank you," I mouthed the words to Jennifer then glanced at the clock. "Oh no. We've got less than fifteen minutes to clean this mess up and be in our rooms for bed checks. Everybody grab something and get out of here."

#

The next twelve days felt like twelve weeks. But finally, on November 25, I sat at my desk addressing an envelope to the girls. On the note inside, I'd written:

> November 26
> Gone to get married.
>
> Morgan

After printing the last girl's name on the envelope, I turned my hand and mind toward a blank sheet of paper. The words didn't come easy. No matter what I wrote, it wouldn't change anything.

> Dear Mom,
>
> By the time you get this note, Chuck and I will be married. We married November 26, in Alabama. The marriage is very legal.
>
> I think every girl must look forward to sharing the dreams of her wedding day with her mother. I'm sorry that wasn't the case for us.
>
> I wish you could be happy for me.
>
> Love,
> Morgan

I sealed it and wrote Mom's name on the envelope. Almost everything had been taken care of, except how to stop Richard from driving up on the twenty-seventh. If I contacted him before

Wednesday morning, it might cause suspicion. And then there was the matter of how to get the note to Mom so she and Dad wouldn't worry when I didn't come home. Mailing it was out of the question, it might not make it in time, and Kyle already refused to hand deliver it. I couldn't blame him, and even though Becky would be going home Wednesday, I wouldn't think of asking her. Oh, well. I opened my top desk drawer and placed the finished envelopes inside. I'd think of something.

#

Becky and I planned to be up by four thirty and out the door to meet Chuck and Kyle as soon as Mrs. Henderson unlocked it and turned off the alarms at six.

Throughout the night, all kinds of emotions coursed through me: joy, love, happiness, giddiness, and yes, some fear of how my parents would react. I couldn't sleep. By four, I tossed back the covers and bounced out of bed. I grabbed the tote bag packed with everything I'd need for the day, including the dress from Janet and her mother, and my coat. The corners of my lips curved upward as I hurried to the shower room.

I sang "The Wedding Prayer" softly while showering and enjoyed the sound of my own voice sending a personal petition to God. After drying off, I held my wedding dress and fondled the detailed stitching and beautiful material. I hugged it and thanked God for my lifelong friend, Janet.

I eased my feet into my shoes and tugged my coat over the white outfit in case someone walked in. After brushing my teeth and fixing my hair, I removed my makeup kit.

The door opened, and Jennifer sauntered past me yawning, scratching her head, and sliding her slippers against the floor with every step. She reached for the stall door, then stopped and did an about-face. Without saying a word, she closed in on me and began circling, forcing me to step back. Again, she circled. With her hands on her hips and stifling laughter, she scanned me from head to toe. "What are you doing?"

"Nothing. Just getting an early start on the day." I couldn't contain a smile any longer.

She snorted and inspected my feet. "This is it. You're getting married today."

"Why would you think such a thing?"

"Oh, I don't know," she glanced down again, "maybe it's your shoes."

"What's wrong with my shoes?" I stuck out my foot.

"They're white, honey. Nobody wears white shoes after Labor Day. Unless, of course, they're getting married."

"Okay." I lowered my voice as if others were in the room. "Today's the day. I was going to leave a note for y'all, letting you know."

She focused on my head and shook hers. "We've got to do something with that hair."

I glanced in the mirror and back at her. "It's fixed already."

She lifted a strand here, another there. "Maybe for school, but not for today. No way. Trust me. I'm not *about* to let you go off and get married with your hair looking like that."

"Jennifer, if anyone comes in here and catches you whipping up one of your stylish dos, we might as well announce my plans over the intercom."

"Get your stuff and come on."

I picked up my tote bag as Jennifer grabbed everything else. "Where are we going?"

"To the lounge. No one ever goes in there this time of morning."

I'd hardly walked through the lounge door, and Jennifer pushed me down in a chair and went to work. I watched in a small makeup mirror as she teased, sprayed, lifted, and molded my hair into the picture of perfection, with a bold side fringe that swept my left cheek. "Go stand over there, and let me survey the finished product."

I stood and sashayed over to the window and struck a pose.

Jennifer laughed. "I sure wish the girls could see you."

"Wait right here. I'll be back." I opened the door to leave.

"Morgan."

"What?" I asked over my shoulder.

"Don't forget your penny loafers. Those shoes you have on are a dead giveaway."

I slipped out of my shoes and ran down the hall in my stocking feet, retrieved the envelope addressed to the girls from my desk and loafers from my closet, then rushed back. I handed the envelope to Jennifer. "Will you read it whenever you're all together?"

"Sure, and I'll tell them what a beautiful bride you made. Oh, honey, that Chuck's a lucky guy."

My smile widened. Luck had nothing to do with me and Chuck. God had answered our prayers.

"Thanks for everything, Jennifer." I gave her a quick hug and turned to leave, hiding my white shoes under my coat. Becky would be waiting for me on the first floor stairway.

"We'll miss you."

I smiled. "You won't have a chance. I'll be back before bed checks."

From the stairwell, Becky and I listened to Mrs. Henderson fiddle with the door. We waited for her retreating footsteps before Becky walked into the hallway and signaled. When we opened the side door, Chuck stood there, tall and proud in his brown pinstriped suit. He grabbed my hand and raced toward a blue Chevrolet.

"Whose car?" I scanned the parking lot for anything or anyone out of the norm.

"Marvin's. We swapped. I thought in case your parents had someone keeping an eye out for us, they might not recognize his car."

Becky jumped in the front seat with Kyle. Chuck and I climbed into the back.

I shed my coat and snuggled next to him.

He touched the side of my face with his left hand. "You're beautiful, your dress, your hair…"

"Thanks—your arm! You got your cast off."

"Doc removed it yesterday." He flexed his hand, leaned over the front seat, and then presented me with a bouquet of daisies. "These are for you."

A wide, green, satin ribbon held the stems. "They're beautiful, and my favorite."

"Yes, I know." His arms tightened around me.

"Okay, has anyone forgotten anything?" Kyle asked. "Speak now or forever hold your peace, because this wedding party's heading out."

Chapter 21

Two hours later, we stopped in Danville. It was thirty minutes from our hometown and the most nerve-wracking point of the trip. We could run into someone we knew, but Chuck's father promised to meet us there.

"Where's your dad?" I scanned the parking lot once more for Mr. Mathew's red Ford pickup. "He's not here." My chest tightened. I spun around. "Are you sure he said Texaco? There're other services stations farther down? Should we—"

Chuck squeezed my hand. "It's okay, Morgan. Don't worry. He'll be here."

But without him to sign for Chuck, there would be no wedding.

After filling the car with gas, Kyle thought to drive around back. There Mr. Mathews sat, his head resting on the back of the seat with his hat over his eyes. I exhaled as Chuck got out and tapped on his window. In a matter of minutes, we were on the road again, headed to Vernon, Alabama.

The trip to Vernon went by fast. Mr. Mathews shared various stories about Chuck's childhood: his first job delivering eggs at age eleven, his first bicycle, purchased from selling a runt pig he'd raised, and their many hunting trips. He even slipped up and called him by his nickname, Cooter. Chuck swore he didn't know where the name came from. His father chuckled but never divulged the secret.

By ten fifteen, Chuck and I stood in front of the powers-that-be applying for a marriage license. I held my breath and prayed we had all the necessary papers. Afterward, Chuck phoned the preacher to confirm the time, and then Kyle drove us all to a small restaurant for lunch.

A battalion of grasshoppers were at war in my stomach. I refused to order anything to eat. I had no doubts about marrying Chuck, but anyone who gets married and says they're not nervous isn't normal. I nursed a chocolate milkshake, listened to the others' conversations, and waited until time for us to leave.

At twelve thirty-five, we left the restaurant and Kyle followed Chuck's directions to the preacher's house. As we pulled into the driveway, Chuck's eyes probed deeply into mine. "You ready?"

"Yes," I answered with such a huge smile my cheeks hurt.

Chuck tightened his hold on my hand and helped me out of the car. The five of us walked toward a cute white house with black shutters. As we stepped onto the porch, a man opened the door and extended his hand. "I'm Pastor Bill Hayne."

A friendly smile curved into his boyish cheeks—was he really old enough to be a pastor? Inside, he introduced us to his very pregnant wife, Anna. She offered iced tea to the others while Pastor Hayne led Chuck and me into his study. He checked the papers Chuck handed him before turning his gaze and directing his comments toward us.

"Marriage is not to be taken lightly. Marriage is to be held in honor. The vows you take today in front of witnesses, and more important God, are binding. Are you both ready to make a true commitment to one another?"

Chuck glanced my way. "Yes." We responded as one.

After Pastor Hayne prayed for God's blessings on our marriage and guidance in our life, we joined the others in his living room. He told us where to stand. I closed my eyes and inhaled a slow, deep breath. *Lord, please don't let this be a dream.* Then the ceremony began.

"Do you, Morgan Ann."

He said the two names together so fast, it sounded like Morgadan.

"Take Charles—"

Not Chuck?

I wanted to stop him. Correct him. Slow him down. But I reminded myself God knew our hearts, our names, and our future. Instead of concentrating on our names, I fixed my mind on the words of our vows and the importance of the moment. Tears stung my eyes. It was really happening, the miracle I'd prayed for. My hand shook as I held it out for Chuck to place the wedding band on my finger. With his help, I managed to slide the band on his.

Within minutes, Pastor Hayne's enthusiastic voice rang out: "I now pronounce you man and wife."

Chuck grabbed me and swung me around the room before following the pastor's directive, "You may now kiss your bride."

We both laughed then cried. I expected to wake up any second and find out I'd dreamed the whole thing. But with the sharp, bitter smell of the daisies, the hard feel of the wedding band, the ring of Kyle's and Becky's congratulations, and the backslap of Mr. Mathews welcoming me to the family, it couldn't be. If it were a dream, it was the nicest I'd ever had. One I never wanted to end.

#

Twelve hours after leaving the dorm, Kyle, Becky, Chuck, and I arrived back in Waitsville, outside the little white house we would call home.

Chuck carried me across the threshold while Becky snapped the picture.

"Perfect. Now you two stand over there." She pointed toward the couch. "And I'll get a picture of Chuck removing your garter."

"*Becky.*" I glared at her then drew my lips tight.

"Hey, I'm all for that." Chuck dropped down on one knee. "Which leg?"

I turned my back, so neither he nor Kyle could see what I was doing, and eased the garter down above the hemline. "Okay, Becky, get ready." I pivoted and rested my right foot on Chuck's leg, then pointed my finger at him. "Behave yourself."

He wiggled his eyebrows at me. Then with his gaze fixed on mine, he let his hand migrate up my leg and remove the frilly, elastic band. He twirled it around his finger while Becky got another shot.

"I believe it's customary for the groom to give that item to his best man."

Chuck placed it over both index fingers and flung it toward Kyle slingshot style. Kyle looped it around his ear.

"Here." Chuck took the camera from Becky. "Stand over there with Kyle so I can get a picture of you two."

In all our planning, I'd never once thought about pictures and how priceless they'd be someday.

After a few more pictures, Becky and Kyle congratulated us again and, without warning, announced their plans to leave.

"But it's early yet." A part of me wanted to beg them to stay.

"I'm sure the girls are dying to hear all about the ceremony and that you are now officially Mrs. Chuck—excuse me, Mrs. Charles

Jefferson Mathews."

"Don't forget to explain why I have to come back to the dorm tonight. And Becky," I leaned close and whispered, "tell them not to ask me a lot of questions about tonight. Okay?"

Chuck interrupted, "You've both got this phone number. If Morgan's parents show up or you find out they've called, or anything out of the ordinary happens…"

"Don't worry, buddy. I've decided to crash at Panola Hall with Jim and some of the guys. We'll let you know if anything comes up." Kyle held out his hand. "Thanks for letting me be a part of this. You two deserve the best."

Chuck draped his arm over my shoulders. "I've got the best."

We stood in the doorway as they drove away, leaving Chuck and me—for the first time—all alone as husband and wife. Surprisingly, the reality of it all scared me much more than I ever thought it would.

After locking the door, Chuck stepped closer, pressing his body against mine. "We've waited a long time for this day, haven't we?"

My head rested against his chest. "Um hum."

"Are you nervous?"

"Petrified," I confessed, too embarrassed to look at him.

He lifted my mouth to his. "I love you, Morgan." Then he wrapped me in his arms.

Again and again we kissed, both of our bodies responding to the other's. Only this time, there was no stopping. The warmth of his hand caressed the back of my neck. I flinched as he began to unzip my dress.

Then in one quick swoosh, he swept me up in his arms and headed into the darkened bedroom.

My heart did a nervous flip-flop when my feet touched the floor and he slowly began to slip the dress from my shoulders.

"It's okay, Morgan," he whispered against my mouth as if he knew I needed to be reminded we were married.

His fingers laced with mine as he gently lowered me to the bed. Soon the warmth of our bodies meshed together, claiming God's gift of marriage. The healing balm of love faded everything else from my mind. For in that moment, other than the two of us, no one or nothing else existed.

#

Harsh phone rings jolted me awake.

Chuck bolted out of bed, hopped on one foot and then the other, pulling on his pants. "It's all right," he tried to assure me before jogging down the hall toward the kitchen and the ringing phone.

How could this have happened? How could we have fallen asleep? I tossed the covers back and frantically began to dress.

He walked back into the bedroom. "That was Becky. We've got to get you back to the dorm."

My legs and hand shook uncontrollably. "Are my parents—?"

Chuck placed his hands on my shoulders. "No. But we've got to hurry."

"Why? What time is it?" I twisted around, frantically trying to find a clock.

"It's after ten."

"Ten!" I pulled away from him. "I can't go back. The dorm mother's already locked the door and called them. We've got to get out of here. We've got to—"

"Listen to me." He placed his arms around my waist and held on tight. "Becky's talked Mrs. Henderson out of doing anything for now, but she told Becky she couldn't wait much longer."

"But what if—"

"If we get there and find out anything different, I won't leave you there."

He helped me get in the car, and we headed toward the campus.

My whole body jerked in uncontrollable spasms.

"If we have to, we'll drive to Memphis. You're my wife now. Neither your parents, nor anyone else will ever hurt you again. I promise." His voice cracked. "If I'd had any idea your dad—"

"Don't." The word vibrated through clattering teeth.

We drove the rest of the way in silence. Each caught up in our own thoughts. As soon as we stopped in front of the dorm, I opened the car door to get out, but my legs wouldn't hold me. I fell to my knees. He reached around my waist and lifted me to my feet.

"Don't let go of me."

"I've got you, Morgan."

The door opened. Mrs. Henderson stepped out and helped him get me inside and seated in a chair. My body continued to jerk in spasms. The tears wouldn't quit flowing.

"Have her parents been called?" he asked.

"No. It goes against everything I've ever done, but I haven't called them."

"Are you going to?" His tone was firm.

She looked at me and shook her head. "No. I'll have to write you up, Morgan, and you'll have to go before the Dean of Women after Thanksgiving break."

All I could do was nod.

Mrs. Henderson turned to Chuck. "I'll have to ask you to leave now."

"I need a minute with Morgan," he responded.

"My patience has been tried enough for one night. You need to leave. Now."

He ignored her, knelt beside me, and took my hands in his. "You don't have to stay."

My chattering teeth made it difficult to answer. "Yes. I do." It was best. The lawyer had said twenty-four hours. But no one should ever have to spend their wedding night separated from their spouse, with their emotions shredded.

"I'll be here tomorrow before your last class. If you need me before then, call me—no matter what time of day or night. You hear me?" He held my hands between his.

I nodded.

He leaned in and kissed me.

Before Mrs. Henderson could protest our public display of affection, he stood and faced her. "I appreciate you not calling her parents. You have no idea what she's been through. I thought I did before tonight, but even I had no idea how bad…" He searched my eyes, as tears welled in his, and mouthed, "I love you."

A tear escaped and ran down his face.

"She'll be fine. I'll get some of the girls to help get her to her room."

"We'll help, Mrs. Henderson," Jennifer called out as she, Becky, Ann, and Wendy rounded the corner of the hallway.

The dorm mother placed a hand over her eyes. "I've lost complete control of this building." Her voice no longer contained a sense of calm and gentleness. She strode to the door and held it open, then nodded to Chuck. "Leave now, before I'm forced to call more than her parents."

I tried to force a smile as he backed out the door. We kept eye contact until the door finally closed. As though a large, invisible hand reached inside my chest and squeezed out the last drop of blood, I sat paralyzed and drained of life.

Wendy and Jennifer each took an arm, placed it over their shoulders and around their neck, and then raised me to my feet. We headed for the stairway with them doing most of the work.

Mrs. Henderson asked, "Are you sure you girls can manage?"

"We're fine," Wendy responded.

"We'll never get her up the stairs," Becky whispered and waited for the dorm mother to leave. "Let's take her to my room. It's closer, and I'd feel better if she stayed with me tonight."

"You'll get written up," I warned.

"I don't care. The bed's big enough to hold us both."

"Her teeth are chattering something awful. I think she's cold. Maybe a hot shower would warm her up and help calm her," Ann suggested.

"That's a good idea. Jennifer, why don't you and I help get her in the shower—"

"No!" Becky and I both answered.

Becky drew in a deep breath before continuing more calmly, "Here. Let her lie down for a while first."

Mimi hovered around and placed one of her blankets on top of me. "Have you had anything to eat? I can make you some hot chocolate or get you something out of the machine."

I thanked her and waited for the multiple questions I was sure she'd have for me. They never came.

Later, after I showered, Becky and I lay in bed. "I got some great pictures today. I'll get them developed this weekend."

"Thanks for everything. I don't know how you talked Mrs. Henderson out of calling my parents tonight."

"It wasn't easy. I was sweating."

"And thanks for talking the girls out of helping me with a shower…I couldn't allow them to see…you know," I whispered softly even though Mimi's slow steady breathing indicated she must be asleep.

"I didn't figure you needed to explain the condition of your back to them."

"No, I didn't. It was hard enough when Chuck saw the scars."

"What did he say?"

"Oh, Becky, it was awful." I could still see his face. "He didn't notice at first—everything was so dark and all. But later, in the bathroom, he walked in and caught me by surprise."

"And saw what I saw?"

"He traced each one with his finger and cried, apologizing over and over as though it was all his fault."

"I bet he's pretty angry at your parents?"

"I don't know. Chuck doesn't have much of a temper."

"Maybe he'll understand now why you've always been so afraid, and why they've had such control over you."

Unable to sleep, I laid awake, thinking about the love Chuck and I had shared tonight as husband and wife. The room had grown quiet. I was sure Becky had finally drifted off to sleep.

"You know, Morgan…"

I jumped at the sound of her soft voice.

"… I'd never guess you and I would be sleeping together on your wedding night." She sniggered softly.

I knew she wanted to lighten the moment, but I bit my lip to keep from crying and said nothing.

Chapter 22

While Becky and Mimi slept, I eased out of bed and folded the covers over where I'd laid. Mimi's nightlight allowed me to locate my house-shoes without getting on all fours.

Becky propped up on her elbow and rubbed her eyes. "Where're you going?"

"Sorry. Didn't mean to wake you."

"Are you too excited to sleep?" she whispered.

"Yes, and nervous. I still need to get in touch with Richard and do something about the note I wrote Mom."

"Why didn't you mail the thing?"

I sat on the edge of her bed. "Because, if for some reason it got there too early—"

"Then they might have stopped the wedding."

"Exactly."

Becky eased herself up in bed and braced her back against the wall. "Listen, since your first class starts at eight, and mine doesn't start until nine, I'll call Richard."

"And tell him what?"

"How about if I tell him you're leaving with someone else? It's the truth, and I don't have to give my name."

I played the scenario over in my mind. "What if he recognizes your voice?"

"He won't, darling," Becky drawled with exaggeration.

I slapped my hand over my mouth to suffocate a burst of laughter.

"And don't worry about the note," Becky continued. "I've got that all figured out, too."

My amusement stopped cold. "What are you going to do? Waltz in the store and say, 'Here you go, Mrs. Selby. A note from your daughter. By the way, congratulations, she and Chuck are married.'"

"I'm not that brave *or* stupid. But does the thing have to be hand delivered?" She shrugged. "I mean, I could tape the envelope to your parents' front door or put it under the windshield wiper of their car, wouldn't that work?"

"I don't know, Becky. I love you for wanting to help…"

"Then let me." She scooted closer. "This way, you can stop fretting and enjoy the next few days."

I reached over and hugged her. "All right. I'll bring the note and Richard's number."

"You won't have to." She beamed.

"What do you mean?"

"They're in my desk drawer. I took them out of your room yesterday."

My mouth hung open. I couldn't picture Becky snooping through my things. "And what if I hadn't agreed to your plan?"

"Then I wouldn't have told you where they were." She nudged my shoulder. "Now stop worrying, and get ready to enjoy your honeymoon."

"Oh, if only Chuck and I could leave right now, but the professors made it clear—for every class missed—we get a zero.

Otherwise, I'd skip today entirely."

"You and me both," Mimi Clair's voice rang loud and clear.

I twisted around so fast, I almost fell in the floor. Mimi stretched her arms above her head and yawned.

"I'm sorry, Mimi. Did we wake you?" I asked, trying to appear calm.

"Nope. I've been awake."

I sucked in my bottom lip and glanced at Becky. Mimi rolled over and turned her back to us. What had she heard? At this point, what did it matter?

"What time do you and Mimi plan on leaving for Greer?"

"Not before twelve thirty or one. Why?"

"I'll see you before then. I'm going to get dressed and tell the girls bye before my first class."

#

Halfway through the last lecture of the day, I'd decided I deserved a zero for each class. I hadn't been able to muster up one bit of interest. The history professor rambled on about dates, places, and people who'd long been dead, when all I wanted to do was live in the present with Chuck.

"Enjoy your time off," barely left the instructor's mouth before I grabbed my books and sprinted toward the door. Out of breath, I spotted Chuck walking toward me.

As he took my books, he leaned in for a kiss.

I put my hand on his chest, sure we'd broken enough of Midway's rules. "We're on campus, remember?"

"You know, it's a sad day when a husband can't kiss his wife in public. At least we can hold hands." He laced his warm fingers between mine.

We exchanged flirtatious looks and strolled toward the dorm.

The parking lot was busy with girls hauling luggage and laundry bags to their cars. Then I saw him: Richard Webster swaggered across the pavement, going the opposite direction.

"Chuck!"

"I see him. Did you forget to call?"

"Becky was going to. She must not have been able to get in touch with him."

"He doesn't look too happy, does he?" Chuck stated matter-of-factly.

"Should we say or do something?" But it was too late. Richard reached his car and peeled out of the parking lot.

Chuck tugged my hand. "Come on. There's nothing we can do about it now."

When we entered the lobby, I turned to him. "I'm all packed, but need to talk to Becky. Be right back, okay?"

He settled into a nearby chair. "I'll be here."

After getting my suitcase and saying good-bye to Paige, I headed to Becky and Mimi Clair's room. Clothes were scattered everywhere. Mimi glanced up, but didn't say anything.

Becky tossed a laundry bag on the floor. "Hey, girl. You and Chuck taking off?"

"Yeah, he's waiting on me downstairs. Becky, were you not able to get in touch with Richard?"

She stopped stuffing items in her suitcase and jerked around to face me. "I called him and told him what we'd talked about. Why?"

"Because, I just saw him in the parking lot."

"Maybe he came after someone else."

"I didn't see anyone with him, and the way he squealed out of the parking lot, I'd say he's pretty mad."

"Oh, he's mad all right." Mimi plopped on her bed and started laughing.

Becky turned toward her. “What are you talking about?”

Mimi looked at Becky, then me. “I thought the fink needed to be taught a lesson.”

Becky and I stood there with our mouths gaped open.

“He’s been snooping around for the past three months, asking me all sorts of questions about you, Morgan.”

“What kind of questions?”

“Who you were dating. Had I seen Chuck hanging around? Those kinds of questions. I should’ve told you, but to be honest, I didn’t think too much about it at first. Then when the questions persisted I became suspicious, but by then…well, I didn’t think you’d believe me. Especially after you got the phone call warning someone might be watching you. Between the way you and Becky both acted, always clamming up whenever I came into the room, I got the impression you thought it was me.” Mimi studied her hands. “I figured by then if I said anything, you’d probably think I was trying to divert attention away from me.”

“You’re right. I did think it was you. You were always asking questions: ‘when are y’all getting married, and where.’ And you seemed to pop up at the oddest times.”

“I tried to find out everything and then feed Richard false information. He’s such a dork. He thinks any girl should jump at the chance to date him, and the way he cons the adults…his own father would disown him if he knew what he was really like. But I got him good. I heard y’all talking and planning and knew Becky was going to call him. So I waited until she did and called him back, and told him you changed your mind. That way, he’d drive all the way up here, thinking he’d have the honor of driving you back to Greer.” Mimi held her stomach and howled. “The only thing he’s taking back to Greer is the note you wrote your mother and a piece of my mind.”

Becky walked to her desk and opened a drawer, then turned to me. "She did."

"You gave the note to Richard?"

"Yep. The dude doesn't have a clue what's in the letter unless he opens it. And if he does, so what? He'll still hand deliver it. I don't know if your mother used him to get information about you, Morgan, but if she did, you'll get the last laugh."

I dropped in a chair. "I don't need the last laugh…I don't know what to say." And I didn't. I couldn't believe she'd pulled such a dirty trick on Richard, or he'd had any reason to care about what I did or didn't do. But, more than anything, I hated I'd hurt Mimi by not being honest with her.

I chewed on my thumbnail and tried to think of the right words. All kinds of excuses popped in my head, but that's all they were…excuses. "I'm sorry, Mimi. I hope you'll forgive me?"

The intercom crackled. "Would Mrs. Chuck Mathews please report to the lobby?"

I sprang to my feet. "Oh, no. He's been waiting all this time. Mimi—"

"Forget about it. I don't blame you, Morgan. I probably would've come to the same conclusion. Just be happy." She waved toward the door. "Go. I'd hate to see you and Chuck start your marriage off on the wrong foot."

The three of us hugged and said our good-byes. By the time I made it back to the lobby, Chuck was not so patiently waiting, but we were soon in the car and headed to a destination unknown. At least by me.

#

Once I got it all out of my system by sharing with Chuck about Richard, Mimi, and how badly I felt over the whole mess, I snuggled up close to him and rested my head on his shoulder. I woke as the car slowed and Chuck took an exit off Interstate 55.

"Did you have a good nap?"

Wiping the sleep from my eyes, I nodded. "Where are we?"

"You'll see." He pointed to a small white block building with two rustic gas pumps out front. "We take a left up here, and then we're less than ten minutes away."

A large yellow sign, Sammy's Grocery And Tackle, hung over the door. "Are we going fishing?"

He laughed and put his arm around my shoulders. "We can if you want to."

Around us, bare patches of ground were as orange as a terra-cotta pot. Rolling hills also hinted we'd left the Mississippi Delta. Once we turned off the blacktop, gravel crunched under the weight of the tires. Large stands of long-needled pine stood on both sides of the road.

"Here we are." He stopped in front of a gray wooden cabin with a tin roof aged by the sun and rain. Two majestic oak trees stood guard at each corner, their bare limbs reaching outward as if welcoming us. Beyond them, a thick grove of pine, as far as the eye could see, waved.

I got out of the car and took a deep breath, inhaling the rustic scent of burning wood, pine needles, and red cedar. "I don't know where we are, but I love it and can't wait to see inside."

We walked up wooden steps and entered a large room that served as kitchen and living room. A pool table sat where a dining table belonged. He opened the refrigerator. "Kyle and I tried to think of everything. We've got steaks, hotdogs, ground beef, bacon, eggs, and ham." Then he opened two cabinets to display other bounty. "I hope we didn't forget anything."

He was kidding, right? No way could we ever eat so much.

"When did you two do all this?"

"Monday."

"The same day you got your cast off and swapped cars with Marvin?"

"Yep." His smile widened, as if pleased with himself. And rightly so.

"You were a busy fellow."

"I tried." He curled his arm around my waist. "Come see the rest of the place."

The little cabin was adorable. A screened-in back deck provided a great view of the lake. The bathroom had an old claw-footed tub big enough for two or three people to bathe in at the same time. I stifled a giggle at the thought of us trying it out later.

In the larger bedroom, he handed me the card laying beside a vase of red roses. I flipped open the cream colored card, my heart catching at the words *I'll love you forever.*

He *had* thought of everything.

At twilight, we followed the trail leading to the water. He built a fire on the bank to roast hotdogs and marshmallows. Frogs and whippoorwills serenaded us as we gazed at the stars. By the week's end, I'd even tried my hand at fishing with nothing but a happy heart to show for it. We never saw or heard anyone. It was as if we were the only two humans on the planet. The perfect setting for making unforgettable memories.

Sunday arrived too quickly. He came inside from taking a load to the car. I placed the broom and dustpan in the closet, then looked around one last time. "I could stay here forever."

"We'll be back someday," he promised. "But right now we have a little house in Waitsville waiting on us."

Once we reached Interstate 55, he announced, "I promised my grandmother to bring you by for a visit. It's a little out of the way, but I thought while we were in Greer, we might as well face your parents and get it over with."

I shook my head to the point of becoming dizzy. "No...No!"

He pulled off the road and put the car in park. As he faced me and gathered my hands in his, he spoke calmly, "We can't avoid them forever. They live in the same town as my family. Sooner or later, we'll run into them. I'd rather it be on our terms with us prepared for it."

"You don't understand."

"I understand now more than before we got married. I'll be with you, Morgan. Right beside you. They can't hurt you anymore."

The threatening tears took over and streamed down my cheeks. With all my heart, I never wanted to see them again. The relationship between me and my parents was damaged beyond repair, but out of respect and love for Chuck, I reluctantly agreed. He had to see for himself what Mom and Dad were capable of.

#

Long before we made it to the city limits of Greer, lifelong fearful emotions surged through me, dousing the peace and hope the past five days had brought. Now, surrounded by Chuck's grandmother and his two aunts, I nodded, smiled, and sipped iced tea, hopefully hiding the turmoil raging inside.

"Are you sure I can't get you something to eat?" Chuck's grandmother's kind eyes and pleasant smile reminded me so much of my own Gram.

"No, thank you. I'm—"

"Lock the door and hide the cake." Chuck passed me his empty plat and pushed himself from the couch. "Here comes trouble."

High-pitched squeals and laughter entered the house long

before two little girls scampered inside. Their voices rose several ear-piercing octaves when Chuck jumped from behind the door and grabbed them, winning all three a scolding from their Aunt Helen.

"I can't help it." Bright blue eyes—surrounded by mounds of copper, short, springy curls—peeked from behind her big brother. "He gets me all twisted up inside."

"Yeah," the older of the two agreed.

"Come here. There's someone I want you to meet." He tugged the urchins and bribed them with slices of his grandmother's cake, until they stood in front of me, staring more at their feet than at me. "Beth. Amy. This is Morgan."

I dipped my head, trying to make eye contact. "Which one's which?"

Neither of them said a word. So bashful, so cute, and clearly adored by their brother, they didn't have to. Chuck had already told me all about them. Amy, the youngest—four, curly copper-colored hair, skin as pale as her favorite baby doll. And then Beth—five, freckled faced, long strawberry-blond hair, with arms and legs like Olive Oyl.

I could have spent the rest of the afternoon getting to know them better. But all too soon, Chuck reminded me of the phone call I had to make and led me to his old bedroom. "No one will bother you in here."

He had no idea.

"Would you like me to stay?"

Maybe if he did… I nodded, picked up the phone, and dialed my parent's number.

"Hello?"

I couldn't collect enough courage or the air to speak.

"Hello?" Mom repeated, her voice calm and polite.

"It's me.... Morgan."

"Well, well, it's about time. Where are you?"

"I'm at... We're at Chuck's grandmother's. Chuck thought... W-we thought maybe we should talk."

"It's a little late for that, don't you think? I can't believe what you've done."

What did she want me to say? I cut my gaze up at Chuck. What did *he* want me to say?

"Tell her we can be there in five minutes."

"Mom, Chuck says—"

I heard him," she snapped. "Five minutes."

The dial tone hummed through the line.

Chuck eased the phone from my hand. "They can't stay mad forever." He placed his forehead against mine. "Besides, somebody has to make the first move."

Three minutes later, my stomach rolled at the sight of their house...the place I'd promised myself I'd never return to. I knotted my hands together, yet they still shook.

"Remember, they can't hurt you ever again," he promised.

Neither his words nor my memory verse gave me an ounce of courage. The breath squeezed from my lungs as he helped me out of the car.

Chuck stopped me from opening the storm door leading into the den. Instead he knocked.

"Come in," Mom shouted when he knocked again.

Chuck and I entered, with him firmly holding my hand.

"We're in here," Dad growled.

They sat at the kitchen table.

Chuck tugged me forward. My gaze locked on the cigarette Dad held. He lifted it to his mouth and inhaled. With every step, I watched, knowing that the second he laid it down, his wrath would be unleashed.

"Mr. Selby. Mrs. Selby." Chuck nodded to each of them.

"Let me make one thing clear," Dad started in on us, "the only reason you two are here is because of this woman." He jerked his thumb toward Mom, who sat motionless, glaring at me. He still clutched the cigarette.

Dad scanned Chuck with squinted eyes and took several puffs while we settled in the chairs across from them. Then he placed the cigarette in the ashtray and exploded, using an entire arsenal of horrible words. He even used names no man ever wants to hear about his mother. Chuck's expression never changed. He showed no signs of fear.

Then Dad turned to me. "You've cheated, lied, connived, and God only knows what else. You two deserve one another."

Chuck squeezed my hand.

The small motion drew Dad's attention back to Chuck. "If you and I ever have any kind of relationship, you'll have to come one-hundred percent of the way."

"No, sir." Chuck locked eyes with Dad. "I'm willing to come fifty, but if you and I ever have any kind of relationship, you'll have to come the other fifty."

Dad picked up the cigarette and sucked on it, as if attempting to regain strength, along with nicotine.

"And another thing," Chuck glanced at Mom then back to Dad, "you'll never mistreat my wife again."

Chuck and Dad stared at one another. Dad's face flushed and twisted. Chuck's still showed no signs of anger or fear. A rush of pride surged through me.

"If you have nothing more to say, we'll be leaving now." Chuck stood, pulling me close beside him, and led me out.

Chapter 23

On our six-month anniversary Chuck had something special planned, but he'd only hint, "Dress casual."

I inventoried the closet. "How casual?"

"Well, I'd say jeans, but you don't own any," he hollered from the bathroom.

I'd never thought about it before. Why didn't I wear jeans? I tried to visualize myself in a pair and couldn't. So I removed one of Chuck's Levi's from the hanger, slipped it on, then stood on the bed to get a full view in the dresser mirror.

Rubbing his smooth-shaven face, Chuck ambled into the room and laughed. "What are you doing?"

His aftershave reminded me of sun-dried linen. The bed moved beneath my feet as I wobbled toward him. "What do you think?"

"I think they're about eight inches too long, and if you don't get down from there, you might break your neck."

With a smile, I refused to budge.

He grabbed my waist with both hands and lifted me from the bed to the floor. "Now hand 'em over."

"Make me," I teased and lunged for the door. My right foot remained in place, causing me to lose my balance.

Chuck caught me. His lips twitched. "All right. If that's how you want to play."

He'd firmly planted his foot on a portion of the excess pant leg. I began laughing. "That's not fair. You almost made me fall."

"No, I didn't. I had you. I'll always have you." He drew me close for a quick kiss and a slap to my bottom. "But we've got to get going. We've got a long drive."

I slipped out of his jeans and tossed them on the bed. "Please tell me we aren't going to Greer tonight."

"Okay, we're not going to Greer tonight."

I hoped not.

Since the confrontation with my parents, we'd only been back three times—to pick out and complete a bridal registry, to attend the shower, and to visit at Christmas.

It seemed like the whole town went all out for us. I'd never known a couple to receive so much stuff. Janet said Chuck and I were the Romeo and Juliet of Bradford County. I reminded her their plans didn't work out so well. They both ended up dead.

More precious than the gifts, were the words of one of the women who hosted the shower, "We're doing this for you and Chuck, not your mother." Not that I wanted anyone to mistreat Mom, but I'd always been led to believe, by her, that I held no value or respect in the tiny community. True to her word, the women didn't allow my mom to control the night, but Mom flitted around like we had the perfect mother-daughter relationship. Chuck's mother, on the other hand, said little more than "Hi."

Chuck's kiss on the back of my neck erased the visions and memories momentarily. "Come on, Morgan. Enough primping. You look great."

I did a quick scan to make sure my pants and shirt matched and

I had on the right shoes.

Chuck stuffed his billfold in his back pocket and scooted me out of the house. He'd not forgotten how to open the car door for me—the honeymoon wasn't over.

We headed north on Interstate 55, toward Memphis. I exhaled. "When are you going to let me in on the plans for tonight?"

Chuck smiled and faced straight ahead.

"What's the big mystery?"

Still nothing.

"Okay, fine. I won't ask another question." And I didn't until we arrived in Memphis and he maneuvered the car into the downtown area. Then I sat up and locked the doors. "Are we lost?"

"Nope."

"Chuck, I've sat over here and played along with your secret mission about as long as I can stand it. You need to tell me what you're up to."

"Remember several weeks ago when Marvin and I bragged on Grandmother's cooking? Specifically, her barbeque ribs?"

"Yeah, I remember. I told you I'd never eaten ribs."

"Well, after tonight, you won't be able to make that statement again. You're going to taste the finest barbeque ribs this side of the Mason-Dixon line." He licked his lips. "Yes, ma'am. I've only eaten at Big Daddy's Barbeque once, but it can't be beat."

I studied his face for a hint of teasing. His expression didn't give one.

After taking a right on Beale Street, Chuck slowed and scanned the storefronts. "I think we're getting close."

I still hoped he'd announce, "just kidding." But then I saw it, all lit up in big red, flashing letters: Big Daddy's arbeque. The B no longer glowed.

He found a parking space and pulled in. All excited, he

jumped out of the car, came around to my side, and waited for me to unlock the door. "We're making memories tonight, Mrs. Mathews." He grabbed my hand and escorted me across the street.

I hoped we'd live *through* the night. Some of the storefronts appeared vacant. Streetlights were scarce. A man staggered to the curb and drank from a container covered with a brown paper bag.

We entered an old warehouse-like building and walked down a small flight of stairs. The dim lights obscured the dining area. Still, the pictures of Junior Parker, B.B. King, Muddy Waters, Willie Nix, and others grinned down at me. We scooted past them on wide plank boards, stained dark from years of wear. Blues music drowned out the patrons' voices and laughter. Sweet pungent scents and undetermined spices mixed with burning wood permeated the room.

They had a simple menu: pulled pork, steak, or barbeque ribs. Of course, we ordered ribs. Within minutes, a Ball canning jar of iced tea, extra napkins, utensils, and a plate piled with food sat in front of us. After Chuck gave thanks for our meal and our marriage, we dug in.

One bite, and I was hooked. "Where's the barbeque sauce?"

Chuck swallowed and wiped his mouth. "They're dry rubbed. They don't use sauce."

It didn't make sense to me, but I couldn't dispute the fact that the juicy bite of meat breaking apart in my mouth had the most wonderful, spicy taste. And the baked beans, made up of three different varieties of lentils, had a unique flavor of their own—hot, sweet, tangy, and downright delicious.

"Are you disappointed, Mrs. Mathews?"

I reached over and wiped smears from around his mouth. "Not at all. These last six months have been the best part of my life."

"Glad to hear it." He chuckled. "But I'm talking about the ribs."

"They're perfect, too."

#

November 20, six days before our first-year anniversary, the Senate passed Nixon's draft lottery plan. Many referred to it as Nixon's lottery scheme, which did nothing to calm my raveled nerves.

I didn't understand it all. Chuck kept telling me not to worry and reminded me that God was in control. "We'll be fine," he'd say whenever I'd ask questions.

Then on December 1, 1969, the lottery system, to determine the order of men born between 1944 and 1950 to be called up for military service in Vietnam, aired live. We sat glued to the TV. One by one, a capsule, holding a month and day, 366 in all, were drawn from a large glass container. The first capsule contained September 14. The date was then placed on a large board in the number one spot.

God, please, don't take Chuck from me, I cried silently to myself. A prayer I'd prayed for weeks.

As they announced each date and placed it on the board, I remembered to breathe, thanked God, and continued to pray. Then the sound of a man's voice reading, "October twelfth," took me to my knees. The TV blurred as he posted Chuck's date of birth in the seventy second spot.

I reached for Chuck. He got up and turned off the television, then pulled me from the floor and held me close. We didn't say anything. We didn't have to. Vietnam was inevitable.

Chapter 24

How could anyone watch our military men—dirty, afraid, mangled, or dead—then with the flip of a hand, turn the visions off with the TV? I hadn't watched the news in months. The images ran nonstop in my mind.

The second week of December, Chuck came home from work and tossed his lunch pail on the kitchen counter. "I've given my two weeks' notice. I don't know how soon I'll get my orders, but I've got to get you settled in Greer."

Anger seethed inside me much like a bottle rocket. Only for me, the fuse had lit the first night of December. "Don't you think you should've talked to me first? I'm not moving. I've got a job…"

He reached for my hand and rubbed its back. "You can't stay here, baby. You don't make enough money. Besides, I've got to know you'll be okay and with family…my family."

I jerked away from him and began to cry. "I'll get another job. I'll get two! But I'm *not* moving to Greer. This is our home, and when you come back, it'll still be our home."

Chuck pulled out his handkerchief and led me to the couch. He held me until the tears subsided, yet the anger continued to fester. I wasn't mad at Chuck. I was mad at God.

Chuck brushed a strand of hair from my face. "I've already talked to Grandmother. She's eager for you to move in with her. You can stay in my old room."

I shook my head and sat up straight. "I can't. I don't really know your grandmother, and she doesn't know me. Besides..." My thoughts raced. Why couldn't he understand? "Have you forgotten my parents also live in Greer?"

"No, but they can't hurt you now. You know that, and so do they."

"Please," I begged. "There's got to be another way."

He sighed. "Okay...Grandmother has a shop in her backyard. There's running water, a bathroom, and with a little bit of work, I can turn it into an efficiency. With the money I'll send home and whatever job you can find, you'll be able to make it while I'm gone. The shop sits between her house and my parent's, so you won't be lonely."

"You want to bet?" I huffed.

He leaned closer. "Please don't fight me on this. I don't like it any more than you do. You think I want to leave you?" His eyes reddened. "It'll be hard, but we'll get through it. We always have, haven't we?"

Torn between my desires or his, I buried my head against his chest and refused to answer. How could he think about moving me to Greer? Or that I wouldn't be lonely? After several minutes of silence, I finally gave in. "Okay. Whatever you say."

The next morning, I explained our circumstances to Mr. Perkins and gave my two weeks' notice. He shook his head and walked away without saying a word.

At first, I thought he was angry with me, but then Betty explained, "His nephew was killed in Vietnam last year. He hasn't gotten over it."

My stomach twisted in knots.

By the second week in January, Chuck, with the help of his father, had refurbished the little shop. We moved in with bare necessities and stored everything else at his grandmother's. The tiny kitchen held a twenty-four inch range, a white 1950s refrigerator, and a metal cabinet-sink combination. A double bed, dresser, and small closet were on the opposite end, leaving enough room in the middle for two chairs and a TV. The only private spot was the bathroom, where a person could sit on the toilet, wash their hands, and soak their feet all at the same time. One of Chuck's aunts gave us a roll of orange, shag carpet, left over from her "Latest remodeling adventures." The floor covering, along with the dark paneled walls, made the living quarters look like a dungeon. It matched my feelings of despair.

I found a part-time job at an auto parts house, keeping books four hours a day, six days a week. Chuck went back to work for Mr. Fisher.

I couldn't hope to avoid my parents since we all went to the same church. The one I'd attended since birth. The one whose members had made a major impact on my knowledge of God. But my dad, the deacon, who went out of his way to welcome people, never once acknowledged our presence. Oh, he'd nod if Chuck or I spoke, but nothing more. I often wondered if the shunning would last a lifetime and tried to convince myself it didn't matter.

The first time I shopped at their store, Dad busied himself, following one of the older widow ladies around, gathering items she rattled off from her list. His smile reminded me so much of his mother's...my mamaw. His smile vanished when he saw me.

Chuck's words, *they can't stay mad forever*, played over in my mind as I read from my own list. Not that I'd forgotten what was on it, but I'd never been able to meet Dad's intimidating gaze.

I picked up a 30 amp fuse Chuck's dad sent me after and placed it in the basket next to the washer for the kitchen sink. Then I flipped the efficiency key over in my palm. We needed another key, and it wasn't as if I didn't know how, or hadn't cut duplicates before, but I didn't dare. Not anymore. Instead, I dropped the key inside my purse, and after a swift kick to the wobbly front wheel that locked up for the fourth time, headed to the next isle to pick out a whole-new doorknob—keys and all. The cheapest one cost much more than I'd anticipated. But so had the emotional toil of being in the presence of my parents without Chuck. I tossed the package in with my other articles and made my way to the front counter.

Mom didn't say a word as I unload my buggy.

"Busy day?"

"Humph, every day's busy around here." She inspected my items, then leaned over and looked inside the crippled cart. "Is that it?"

The tightness in my throat increased. "Yes, ma'am."

"We heard y'all had to move back." She punched numbers on the monstrosity cash register. "I also hear Chuck's waiting to be drafted. A few years in the military will probably do that boy a lot of good. He's got a smart mouth on him."

Her words sliced through me with the precision of a skilled surgeon, but I clamped my mouth shut. I wouldn't be back. They might have the only hardware store in town, but there were other towns.

We'd hardly gotten settled when the official notification came. Chuck was being drafted and called up for a physical. I prayed they'd find a problem. Nothing life threatening. Maybe a heart murmur or only one kidney. Something. Anything. But he passed. They classified him 1A.

A week later a letter came. Chuck tore it open while I finished the breakfast dishes and feigned disinterest.

"Well, the wait's over."

My hands gripped the dishcloth. "When?"

"The end of March." He stood beside me. "We have thirty days."

Thirty days? "It's not enough." I threw the wet cloth against the wall. "It's not—"

He opened his arms and wrapped me in their warmth. So close, and yet I missed him already.

The days past much too fast. "There's so much I need to tell you," Chuck kept saying. He talked to me about our finances. Together we wrote out all the bills. "My mother taught me this trick when I bought my first car. This will help you stay on top of things." Chuck labeled envelopes: electric, phone, gas, insurance, groceries, repairs, miscellaneous. He marked each one with a specific amount I'd need to put in weekly and then placed a manila envelope in the top dresser drawer. "This contains all our important papers."

One of them was his life insurance policy. He taught me how to change a flat and check the oil. Almost every day he thought of something else I needed to know or learn.

A week before he left, his family planned a cookout. A mini family reunion, they called it. A chance for everyone to say good-bye. We wanted to spend every moment together, alone.

Marsha and Bob, the only members of my family invited, drove in from Arkansas. It was good to see them. I hadn't realized I missed spending time with Marsha. Her being the big sister, I'd hoped—no, I expected her to share words of comfort, maybe say something to help me make sense out of it all. She'd always been witty, tough, and savvy. I'd admired those qualities and often wished I could be like her. But what if she didn't offer any insightful tidbits? Perhaps only God could help me, but He wasn't talking. Or maybe I couldn't hear Him. I felt His presence and knew I'd never make it without Him, but once again, whys with no answers plagued my life.

With the threat of rain, along with one of March's forty-degree cool snaps, Chuck's grandmother volunteered her home. And soon the large clan, seemingly undaunted by the weather, began to arrive. Aunts, uncles, cousins—even great-aunts and uncles—babies, teenagers, and every age in-between crowded the three-bedroom house, turning the place into a venue of chaos with infants crying, children running in and out, and everyone talking at the same time. I stood back, amazed by all the hugs and laughter. And the fact they cared enough about one of their own to come at all.

Older women wove through the tiny kitchen space as if prompted by some unwritten work assignment. "We've got it, Morgan." Chuck's Aunt Helen dried her hands on her apron, adding pickle juice to the already flour-dusted sunflowers. "I'll call you if we need anything—oh!" She flitted away as the stove timer screeched.

Marsha and I scooted out of her way. "But we don't mind helping. Really."

When she didn't respond, we backed farther into the doorway to avoid disrupting their structured flow.

"Come on." Marsha tugged my shirttail. "Find your jacket and let's get out of here."

I twisted, trying to spot Chuck. I hadn't seen him since his cousin Bill ordered him, along with Bob, to join some of the guys in the living room. "And go where?"

"For a walk."

There! He sat smiling. Laughing. Surrounded by loved ones. If only for a brief moment he could escape the reality of what the next few days would bring, the day would be a success, wouldn't it?

Marsha tapped my shoulder. "It'll do us both some good. We won't be gone long, and who knows, maybe by the time we get back, the ladies may have found something for us to do. At any rate, perhaps it'll take your mind off of things for a while."

I dropped back on my heels. A diversion *would* be nice. "You're right." She'd always been right about so many things. "Let's go."

Outside, savory smoke teased my appetite.

"Where are you girls headed?" Coals sizzled as Marvin slathered his grandmother's homemade barbeque sauce on the seared chicken pieces.

"We thought we'd go for a short stroll." My mouth watered as I resisted the temptation to stick my finger in the sauce dish. "But if you need some help...."

"Nah." He raised the top on the next grill. "Uncle Steve and I've got this covered...if he ever gets back here with more sauce and a fresh cup of coffee for me. Y'all go ahead. Enjoy your walk."

We'd hardly made it past Grandmother's driveway when Marsha asked, "Have you ever thought about having a family? I mean *really* thought about it?"

"Some." But truth be told, I was in no rush. "Why do you ask?"

"I've read and studied enough child psychology to know history sometimes repeats itself. Learned behavior plays a major role in our lives. Too often, the very things we hated about the way we were raised will be what we'll pass on to our children. We become our parents." She placed her hands on her stomach. "And that scares me."

"Marsha." I caught her arms and halted our steps. "Are you pregnant?"

"Yep."

"Why do you say it like that? I'm excited! I'm going to be an aunt. You should be excited."

"I was…. I am." She forced a smile. "Bob and his parents are ecstatic."

"Then what's the problem?"

"Do you know what Mom said when Bob and I told her about the baby?" Marsha didn't wait for an answer. "She pointed at my stomach and said, 'That child will grow up some day and break your heart,' and how I'd 'count the days until it grew up and left home.' I told her I just hope I didn't break my child's heart or spirit. Then I stood there hoping she'd say one more word, but she walked away. I can't imagine being like her or Dad, but it's not like we've had the best role models."

"Sure we did. Gram loved us, took us fishing, hiking, to church. Every summer, we couldn't wait to spend time with her. Life was an adventure. She never raised her voice or hand. There's your role model."

Marsha looked at me sideways. "You haven't seen Gram since she's moved in with Mom and Dad, have you?"

"No. That's one place I've tried to avoid."

"She looks awful. Mom mocked at my concerns, and Gram denies anything being wrong. But something's not right."

"I should go by sometime when Mom and Dad aren't there and check on her. She has to be lonely. Chuck hasn't left yet and already I think I know how she feels."

"Why did you come back here, Morgan? We always said if we ever left this place, we'd never come back."

I kicked a small rock, sending it down the road. "Yeah, I know. And I'm too numb or dumb to even pretend I have the answer to that question, other than I don't want Chuck worrying about me."

#

With only days before he left, Chuck devoted almost all his time to me, but he'd promised to meet Mr. Fisher for lunch Monday. Knowing Mom and Dad would be at work, I picked up two orders at the local dairy bar and headed to see Gram. I walked in smiling.

She sat on the couch wiping tears from her face.

"Gram!" I practically threw the sack of food and my purse on the coffee table and dropped to the couch beside her. "What's wrong?"

She fumbled for the tissue in her pocket, dabbed her face, and blew her nose. "Oh, don't pay any attention to me." She waved her hand and displayed a half smile. "Where did you come from? I didn't hear you drive up."

I pointed toward the bag of food. "I thought we'd have lunch together. Are you hungry?"

Her eyes brightened, and her smile widened. "Daw'lin, I could eat the legs off the table."

"I'll take all this stuff to the kitchen and fix us some iced tea." Before picking up the items, I gripped Gram's frail hand. "But first, tell me what's wrong."

"Nothing." She patted my hand. "I'm fine. You know how old folks get. They cry one minute and laugh the next. It's part of living."

She wasn't going to tell me, but I knew at that moment she needed me as much as I needed her.

#

The day Chuck left for basic training was worse than anything I'd ever experienced. I tried to store the memory of his lips on mine—the warmth, the gentleness, the way my heart responded to his touch, and the tingling current that ran through my body. I looked into his blue eyes wanting to memorize every detail. His arms circled me and held me close, making me feel like our bodies could melt and absorb into one. When the moment came for him to step inside the bus, I dug my fingernails into my palms and fought an urge to run after him or scream out like an injured animal. I forced a smile, but couldn't control the tears. I lost sight of him and only saw figures mingling. The windows glittered through the sudden sheen of tears. The bus door closed with a swish. The motor roared.

A window opened and Chuck's face appeared. "I love you, Morgan!"

I stood dazed and watched him hold his hand high as the bus drove away. I blinked away the tears and tried to keep the dingy, white bus in focus until—he was gone.

The tears wouldn't stop. The road remained a constant blur as I drove home. Back at the efficiency, I locked the only door and pulled the curtains on both windows. A desperate loneliness gripped me.

God, I can't do this! Why wouldn't He talk to me? I reached for my Bible, flopped it open, and began reading.

God is our refuge and strength, a very present help in trouble. Therefore will not we fear, though the earth be removed, and though the mountains be carried into the midst of the sea.

I stopped and reread the first two verses of Psalm 46.

God, my world has been turned upside down. I don't have any strength left. Help me!

Chapter 25

Three days after Chuck left, I drove home from work and found a box on the front steps. My heart fluttered when I recognized his handwriting. What could he be sending? A schoolgirl giggle burst into full laughter as I scurried into the house and tore open the package. I closed my eyes and reached into the box, savoring the moment. My fingers touched fabric. I pictured a dress. Soft cotton, maybe pink, my favorite color. Instead, my mouth slid open as I removed the contents. The pants, shirt, socks, shoes, even the underwear Chuck had worn the last time I saw him, now lay scattered across the bed. He'd been stripped of all reminders of home as if the Army wanted to make a powerful statement. He belonged to them now.

I wrapped my arms around the precious items and hugged them tightly. The faint, familiar aroma of his aftershave intensified my loneliness.

A knock at the door jolted me from my feeble attempts of imagining his arms holding me. I buried my face against his clothing and wiped the tears away, then trudged to the door and opened it.

Chuck's two little sisters thrust handfuls of daffodils at me before turning and running away. At a safe distance, the oldest one stopped and faced me. "Chuck said we should help him look after you while he was away, so you wouldn't be lonely." Then she spun, pigtails flapping, and continued her dash home.

I choked on the words *thank you*. Sobs racked my body. Even in his absence, Chuck was trying to take care of me.

#

Work should have helped fill a portion of the void in my life, but didn't. Men came in, ordered parts, and lollygagged around the counter. Sooner or later, someone always brought up Vietnam. Everyone had an opinion, and sometimes their discussions grew heated and foul.

Today a loud voice rang out, "Did y'all see that mess on the news last night about how many of our men have already died in the war over there in Vietnam?"

An angry voice responded, "I wonder how many more are going to have to lose their lives before President Nixon sees the light?"

"Give the man a chance, Harvey. He's only been in office a few months."

"Try to keep it down, guys. Morgan's in the office," came the owner, Mr. Latham's, voice.

A floorboard creaked. For a moment, no one spoke. Then a deep unknown voice asked, "You think she heard us?"

How could I not? My workspace consisted of four walls without a ceiling. Only the metal rafters and a tin roof kept out the rain. But nothing locked out the dust, which coated everything like dirty snow after a blizzard. Or the rotten-egg odor of a battery being charged or smells of rubber hoses, gasoline, and Gojo—a hand cleaner, every mechanic's cologne.

Every afternoon but Sunday, I put in my four hours and returned to an empty house. The nights seemed never-ending, the mornings maddening. I had too much time on my hands. Last night, an idea popped into my head that I was anxious to share with Gram.

First, I stopped by the efficiency, changed clothes, and reread the letter that came in the morning mail.

Dear Morgan,

I miss you more every day. Most nights, I'm too tired to dream, or I never remember them. But last night, you and I were at home in Waitsville, putting up our first Christmas tree. Do you recall how excited you were when we finished decorating the pitiful thing and I plugged in the lights? You stood there laughing like a little girl while the different colors and happiness sparkled in your eyes. That's the vision I had. The dream was so real. When I woke, I could still feel the warmth of your body as I held you against me. I can hardly wait for the day when dreams become reality again.

Your last letter questioned if I'd heard from Kyle. I haven't. I hope you have by now. I know you're keeping both of us in your prayers.

I've got to go, babe. It's almost time for chow, as they call it. The food could be most anything, and I'd never know it. The Army's teaching us all how to eat without taking the time to taste or chew.

Keep those letters coming. They're the best part of my day.

Forever,
Chuck

The soft tick of the clock penetrated my consciousness. I glanced toward it—five thirty. I slid the letter in its envelope and sprang from the vinyl recliner. I'd have to hurry if Gram and I were to have any time before my parents came home. I jumped in the car and drove much too fast. When I pulled under the carport, Gram stood with the glass storm-door open, peering at me.

"You better slow that car down, young'un. I didn't figure you'd get it stopped before you hit the barn out back."

I snuffed the desire to laugh and stepped into the family room. "Sorry, Gram, but I wanted to make sure we had time to visit."

Her gaze dropped to her gnarled hands. "I wish you'd come see me more often."

I cupped those hands in mine. "Well, I've been thinking about that, and I've got an idea. You know I don't know anything about quilting, but you do. How do you feel about making a baby quilt for Marsha? We could work on it almost every day if you felt like it."

She removed her arthritic hands from mine and held them up. "That was before these fingers got so twisted."

"I can do the work if you'll teach me." I sat on the couch, patted the empty space beside me, and grabbed pen and paper out of my purse. "Come on, Gram. What do you say? Tell me what all we'll need."

The lines around her eyes multiplied as she smiled. I listed everything she suggested and slipped the paper and pen inside my purse. Then I noticed a half empty glass of milk on the coffee table and a tube of broken saltine crackers still sealed.

"Was that your snack today?" I pointed at the mauled package.

"My lunch. But the factories make everything so difficult for people to open these days."

"Gram, have you had anything all day other than milk?"

"I had a bowl of cereal for breakfast. Dot…your mom, opened the box and the carton of milk before she left this morning."

I looked at Gram. Really looked at her. Her spindly legs. The housedress hanging from bony shoulders. Marsha was right. I'd never seen Gram so skinny—why hadn't I noticed sooner?

"You didn't have any lunch?"

She examined the stain on her housedress. "Sometimes I'm not hungry."

"You've got to be starving." I headed toward the kitchen. "I'll fix you something."

She shuffled her feet trying to keep up with me. "That's okay. Dot'll be home before long."

I opened the refrigerator and moved bottles of mustard, pickles, and mayonnaise. Other than the condiments, only an opened can of cat food, a sack of flour, a pitcher of tea, and a dried-up lemon cluttered the shelves.

"What do y'all normally eat for supper?"

"They eat steak a lot. Dot says it's quick and easy. Sometimes she'll bake potatoes. I like them, but I can hardly chew meat anymore. We'll have sandwiches or soup some nights. I guess whatever they decide before leaving town."

I got down on my knees and stuck my head in the corner cabinet where Mom kept canned goods. I nabbed one labeled potato soup and backed my way out. "I'll warm this up for you."

"No, that's okay." Her voice wavered. "Dot might get mad if we mess up her kitchen."

A jolt of panic, like a lightning bolt, struck me. Gram was *afraid* of her own daughter.

"I need to make sure you eat something. I'll clean up everything before I leave. It won't take but a few minutes."

Gram sat at the table while I poured her a fresh glass of milk.

"I remember when Wayne and Marsha and I were young, sometimes Mom would come home in a really bad mood. She'd throw dishes and scream and holler. We never knew why she was so mad." I glanced at Gram as I talked, searching for clues, waiting for a response.

Gram kept her head down. "Dot puts in a lot of hours at work. I expect she's tired."

I placed the warmed soup in front of her with a few crackers. She spooned in the meager supper in a slow but steady rhythm, saying very little while she ate. Once she finished, I cleaned up all the evidence, including what remained on the coffee table.

"I hate to run, Gram, but I've got to go. I'll be back tomorrow." I yanked up my purse and raced to the car. I gripped the steering wheel, backed out of the driveway, and headed home to call Marsha.

She answered on the third ring.

"I'm so mad, I could spit fire." The words spewed from my mouth without the courtesy of announcing who was calling.

"Morgan, what is it?"

"You were right. Something's wrong with Gram. She's starving to death."

"What are you talking about?"

I explained everything: the crying I saw days earlier, the lack of food in the house, the unopened crackers, the conversation. I tugged on the phone cord. "I don't understand."

"Sure you do. You just don't want to admit it."

"But she's her mother, Marsha!"

"And we were her children."

Pain gripped my stomach. "You don't think she'd ever hit her, do you?"

"I don't know why she wouldn't. Let me ask you, do you think our parents have changed?"

Reality smacked me like an open hand.

"Answer the question, Morgan. Do you think our parents have the capability of mistreating a defenseless old woman?"

My hands began to tremble like they hadn't done in months. "What are we going to do?"

"We need to talk to Gram. I'll be at your place Friday night."

#

Gram was so excited when Marsha and I walked in Saturday morning lugging sacks of groceries and the day's lunch. Marsha had purchased things for Gram to keep in her room. Cookies, Hershey bars, peppermint sticks, bananas—the kinds of snacks she'd always had around when we visited her. We ate our meal and stashed the items before sitting down for a serious conversation.

Marsha didn't mince words. "Morgan and I know Mom, and more than likely Dad, are mistreating you. We don't think you need to stay here."

Gram denied it, even after we told how we'd been abused. "Dot's helping me manage my money." Her hands trembled. She wouldn't make eye contact. "I don't know what I'd do without her help and a place to live. It's impossible for me to keep the old home place open."

After coaxing her to confide in us, we learned Mom had full control of Gram's finances, and she intended to inherit Gram's house even though there wasn't a will.

"Dot says before her daddy died, he told her she could have the house." Her voice cracked.

Marsha and I swapped glances and backed off. We talked about the baby and teased about some of the names Bob picked out if he "got his son." Clarence, after his father. Arnold, after one of his grandfathers.

A tear trickled down Gram's face when Marsha announced their choice if they had a girl. "We're naming her after you, Rachael Lee."

With Gram's denial of mistreatment, we couldn't do more than make sure she had food, quality time with people who loved her, and watch for the signs.

Once Marsha and I said good-bye to Gram and got back in the car, I asked, "Why won't she tell us?"

"Why didn't you ever tell?"

"I was afraid."

"That's right, and so is she."

Chapter 26

After Chuck finished basic training, the Army sent him to Fort Benning, Georgia for communication training. He'd be taught how to repair radios in the field. I didn't want to think about what that meant. Instead, I concentrated on the dark wet roads as I traveled between Greer and Meridian, Mississippi. He'd gotten a forty-eight-hour pass and hitched a ride from an Army buddy who lived there.

I slammed on the brakes. My purse and all its contents toppled to the floorboard as the car slid sideways across wet pavement. It took everything in me to stop fighting the steering wheel and simply lift my foot from the pedal. After ten hours of driving—five of them in heavy rain, wind, and darkness—I'd almost missed the turn. It was after one in the morning, forty minutes past the expected arrival time Chuck had predicted. After two more blocks...There! Finally, I spotted the Howard Johnson.

Chuck stood at the entrance pacing under the canopy. When I sighted him, a rush of excitement erased my body's exhaustion.

As I parked beside him, he hurried to the driver's door and opened it. "I've been worried about you." He reached for my hand, practically drug me out of the car, and wrapped his arms around me. "I've missed you."

The breath from his words brushed against my ear, sending a tingling sensation through my body. We clung to each other until thunder shook the air around us.

"Here." He reached in his pocket and handed me a large key. "We're at the end of the hall. Room 142. I'll move the car and bring in your suitcase."

Moments later, Chuck stepped into the room. His drenched uniform lay limp against him. Water dripped from the bill of his cap, adding to the saturated carpet now surrounding him.

"You're soaked! You better get out of those clothes."

He winked as the corners of his mouth turned upward. "Why, Mrs. Mathews, are you trying to seduce me?" Not waiting for an answer, he dropped my luggage and started toward me with his arms open wide. "But first—"

"Don't you dare." I giggled and stepped backward.

We both laughed. Then he grabbed my wrist and pulled me against his drenched body. My free hand pressed against him, playfully protesting, until I connected with the tight muscles in his chest. The change took my breath away.

"Stop it," I squealed, wiggling, trying to break his hold. "You're getting me all wet."

He held me fast, kissing me until his playful teasing filled my lungs with air and the room with laughter. How I'd missed him. My body yielded to his touch, and for the moment, everything that threatened our happiness dissipated.

For the next thirty-seven hours, we basked in the warmth of each other's presence and love. We left the room only to eat or go for short walks.

"Tell me everything," he insisted our first morning together. "How's the job? Mom? Dad? Are you taking good care of yourself?"

I kept my answers light, upbeat.

But then he asked, "What about your folks? Any problems?"

"Not really." I wouldn't have told him any different, even if there had been. "Gram's been a great comfort for me. Remember, I wrote you about how I visit her while Mom and Dad are at work." Telling him about our suspicions would only upset him. Besides, we didn't have any proof. "What about you? Tell me about Fort Benning, your classes, and the friends you've made."

The one subject we both avoided was Vietnam and the real possibility we could be separated for twelve straight months or worse—he could be taken from me, forever.

Sunday, when it came time for Chuck to don his uniform, waves of nausea threatened to expel the breakfast I'd barely eaten. Whoever said a man looked good in uniform must not have envisioned him in combat.

He wiped the tears from my cheeks. "God's going to get us through this. And now that I'm out of basic, there'll be more weekends like this one. Time will pass faster. In less than four months, I'll be home on leave."

And then what? I shook the thought from my mind. My fingers twined with his, holding his hand close to my face. No words would come without a barrage of new tears, so I didn't try to speak. With my eyes closed, I absorbed his warmth.

Chuck slid his hand free. "It's time to go."

My insides twisted. I kept my eyes closed.

"Morgan, look at me."

When I did, he handed me a small box wrapped in shiny, blue paper with the tiniest, white bow. "I bought you something at the PX for your charm bracelet."

I sat on the edge of the bed and removed the paper and lid. A ray of sun reflected from the gold disc. Through tears, I could hardly make out the inscription Separated But Always Together.

He eased down beside me and gathered me in his arms. "We'll always be together, Morgan—in each other's thoughts, hearts, and prayers. No one, not even the Army, can take that from us."

Once again, a steady stream of tears spilled from my eyes. Would there ever be a time when days of smiles and laughter outnumbered the sad ones?

After several minutes, Chuck helped me to my feet. "We've got to go."

Our good-bye ended in reverse of our greeting. In the parking lot, we held on to each other. It reminded me of two little scared monkeys I'd once seen in a zoo. The babies clung to one another as though they were all the protection they had. Unable to understand there was a wiser and smarter keeper who watched over them. I reminded myself we also had a Caretaker. One who keeps a constant vigil, not out of obligation or pay, but because He loves us.

I drove away, watching in the rearview mirror through a sea of tears, wanting one more glance.

#

Days turned into weeks, and life became a little more bearable. Weekend passes and trips to Meridian helped. Even our phone conversations were unrushed since he'd completed basic, his letters longer.

Since school was still out, I had Chuck's little sisters as well as Becky and occasionally Mimi Clair, along with Janet to keep me company. And the time Gram and I spent together kept my hands and mind busy.

Gram and I worked hard on our project and completed all nine six-by-eight white, cotton squares. The blocks came to life, each with a different farm animal cut from materials of unique patterns and colors and hand-stitched in place. Delicate embroidered flowers and leaves framed each little critter. I couldn't believe I'd actually helped make something so beautiful. Nor could I believe the change in Gram. She laughed and talked more and hummed her favorite hymn, "Beyond the Sunset", while she worked. Perhaps Marsha and I had been too quick to jump to conclusions. My conscience twinged, and I winced.

Today, Gram would teach me how to piece the squares together. I dressed quickly, walked to the mailbox to deposit the letter I'd written Chuck last night, and then tossed a bag of groceries into the car. The early morning August heat and humidity had me scrambling to get the air conditioner going full blast. The soaring temperature had taken its toll on the last of the magnolia blooms. But the clusters of blue and pink hydrangeas decorated almost every yard and continued to thrive and show their beauty.

Before pulling into my parent's driveway, I spotted Mom's car parked under the carport. Eight thirty. She must be running late. I had no desire to see her, but a sudden stubborn streak refused to allow me to leave. After parking, I grabbed the sack and stepped onto the gravel. Mom's voice rushed from the house, but I couldn't make out her words. I didn't need to, her tone said it all. I crept closer. Scenes from the past flashed before me. The storm door swung open with a force that jarred me back to the present.

Mom stopped, glared at the sack in my hands, and then at me. "If that's more junk food for Mother's room, you can take it right back to your house. I'm sick and tired of picking up candy wrappers and seeing cookie crumbs on the floor. And another thing, don't leave bits of string and material strewn all over my furniture. I don't know why you two think Marsha would want anything so old fashioned. Why don't you buy your sister something nice...or is money your problem?" Her lips drew into a sneer. "I bet that husband of yours doesn't send home a dime. He probably spends all his money on beer...or whatever he *wants.*"

My face grew hot. My fingers clenched the grocery bag, but I refused to play into her hands. I kept my voice calm. "Who were you hollering at when I drove up?"

"That's none of your business." She stomped toward her car.

"It is if you're mistreating my grandmother."

Mom whirled on her heels and retraced her steps. "I dare you."

Her eyes flickered then narrowed. She didn't blink as I held her gaze. My insides churned. I braced for the blow that never came. Then without a word, she walked back to the car and left, scattering rock and dust as she sped onto the main road.

I took a deep breath and stepped inside. Gram wasn't in the family room, kitchen, or her bedroom. She didn't answer when I called out for her. I knocked on the bathroom door. "Are you in there, Gram?"

No reply. I knocked louder.

"I'll be out in a little while." Her voice quavered, barely audible.

I stood at the door and listened but heard nothing. "I'll start breakfast."

Gram's soft slippers scuffed against the linoleum as I placed a platter of bacon and eggs on the table. She gave me a weak smile when my eyes met her red-streaked ones.

I busied myself pouring coffee and milk, trying desperately to hold in the anger ragging inside.

She ate very little.

"Aren't you hungry, Gram?"

"Some days, I don't have much of an appetite. I'm sorry you

went to so much trouble. Save it, and I'll eat it later on today."

"Yuck. Cold eggs?"

"Young'uns today don't know a thing about the Depression. Back then, you'd be glad to have an egg, hot or cold. Or whatever else you could find. They were good times, but tough ones, too."

"Was it as tough as what you're going through now?"

She didn't look at me or answer.

"I couldn't help but hear Mom when I drove up. Was she upset with you?"

Gram fumbled with the corner of her napkin. "She was running late this morning. That's all."

"Are you sure?"

"It's hard having someone living with you all the time. I'm a burden to her and your dad. I know that."

"Is that what they say?"

Her fingers continued to work the napkin. "They don't have to. I'm of no use to either of them. I can't cook or clean like I used to. What good am I? I'm grateful to have a place to stay."

"You mean the world to me and Marsha. So what if you can't work as hard or as fast as you once did. Who says you have to? You still do a lot. Marsha's going to be tickled when she sees one of your beautiful quilts for her baby. And I couldn't have survived these past months without you. But you don't have to stay here, Gram. You've got other family. And you don't have to be mistreated. I know what it feels like, and—"

"Morgan." Gram raised her head. Her eyes met mine. "You and Marsha shouldn't have ill feeling toward your parents, no matter what they've done or didn't do. You have to forgive and forget and go on with life. That's what the Bible teaches. You know that."

"I know I have to forgive, and I'm working on that. But sometimes, I don't know if it's humanly possible to forget all the hurt."

"If you don't forget, you haven't forgiven."

"Where in the Bible does it say that? …This is hard for me to say, and it's only an example. But, if someone cut one of your fingers off, it would cause a lot of pain. And long after your hand healed, I bet there'd be many times you'd look at your hand with the missing finger and you'd remember. Wouldn't you?"

"I suppose."

"Let's say you forgave the person, and they cut off another finger. According to the Bible, God's word, you'd have to forgive them, but now, with two missing fingers, I doubt you'd soon forget. Maybe over a period of time, you wouldn't dwell on it as much. I don't know. But here's the big question: should you continue to have a relationship with that person, knowing there's a good chance you'll lose yet another finger? Or do you walk away until the person has a change of heart? And if they never do, at least you kept some of your fingers. A pastor in Waitsville gave me this example. It helped me to know what I had to do. Hopefully, it'll help you to know what you need to do."

"Don't worry about me, child. I'm not missing any fingers."

"Gram—"

"That's enough talk. We've got work to do."

#

Later that night, someone knocked on my door. I eased it open. Dad stood on the bottom step. I looked past him. Mom wasn't with him.

"Listen up, girl."

I cringed. "Would you like to come in?" I responded out of upbringing, not desire.

"No. What I have to say won't take long. I understand you talked back to your mother today."

My mouth gaped open. "I did not. I asked her—"

He pointed the fingers holding a lit cigarette in my face. "Shut up and listen! You came to our home this morning, right?"

I swallowed and held my chin up and my shoulders back. "Yes, sir."

"Uninvited. Right?"

"I went to see—"

"Uninvited! Your mother and I know you've been visiting your grandmother while we're at work. If you want to continue spending time with her, I suggest you apologize to your mother for your behavior."

Never blinking, his gaze remained fixed on me, but I refused to look away. "I haven't done anything to apologize for."

He tossed the cigarette to the ground and squashed it with his foot, then leaned inches from my face. "If I ever hear of you talking back to or upsetting your mother again, it'll be the last time you'll step foot in our home. You give that some thought."

He turned and ambled back toward his truck.

The muscles in my arms ached to slam the door off its hinges. Tears stung my eyes. "Don't you dare cry, Morgan Mathews," my voice ordered my heart. I closed the door. "Don't you *ever* allow him to make you cry again."

I thought about calling Marsha to let her know about Dad's threats and today's events. But what could she do? Gram's refusal to open up to us only tied our hands tighter. *God, please. Help us to help her.*

Chapter 27

Two weeks later, a constant influx of men gathered in the parts house with only one thing on their mind, Bradford County's first casualty of the war, Brandon Anderson. His family lived in the small town forty miles south of Greer. I didn't know him or his family. Still, I grieved for their loss. I hated this war. What I really hated was my inability to make sense of it. Civil unrest, and protest against a war many felt we had no business being in, held our country in turmoil. And what seemed a never-ending struggle between the blacks and whites fueled bitterness and anger.

"We can't settle our differences at home," a man with a deep, raspy voice argued. "So why should we think we can help another country reconcile theirs?"

By five that afternoon, my back ached from holding myself stiff trying to ignore the men's talk. My mind screamed for an escape from the little office. I drove out of the parking lot, took a couple of lefts, and steered the car toward home. An empty house would be far better than what I'd endured for the last four hours. In the distance, a yellow Camaro swerved onto the highway. As the car passed going the opposite direction, I shielded my eyes from the sun and craned my neck to get a glimpse of the driver. "Kyle!" I looked for a side road and turned the car around. So many vehicles had passed by, I'd never catch him.

In town, our one and only red light demanded "stop." My patience grew weary waiting for the light to change. Once it did, I scanned Main Street, even cruised past a few of the local hangouts: the dairy bar, Greer's convenience store, and an unnamed clubhouse where men gathered to play cards. I gave up. That's when I spotted his car in the park. Kyle sat on top of a wooden picnic table, black with sap from the surrounding pecan trees. His feet rested on the bench. After a year in Vietnam, he'd made it!

I waved with frenzy as I parked beside his car and jumped out. He stared as though he didn't recognize me.

"Kyle, I can't believe it's really you." I quickened my pace, eager to greet him with a hug. But he didn't stir. He just sat there with his shoulders slumped, holding a burning cigarette. My smile slipped away. "Kyle?"

Finally he spoke, "Hey, Morgan. It's been a while."

"It's been over a year. You stopped writing. Chuck and I wondered if you were getting our letters—"

"I got 'em." He took a drag from his cigarette.

I climbed onto the bench and sat beside him. "Why didn't you write and let us know how you were doing?"

"What was there to tell? That I was still alive?" He smiled...except the smile never reached his blank, bloodshot eyes.

"That would have been nice.... Kyle, what's wrong?"

His smile transformed to a scowl. "Why would there be anything wrong? I've spent twelve months fighting to stay alive. In the States, I've been cursed, spit on, and called a 'baby killer' for wearing a uniform. Idiots who don't know a thing about Nam are marching and protesting." He leaned forward and propped his elbows on his knees. "They don't understand. I'm not sure I do anymore."

Then as though he'd been drawn out of some kind of trance, he straightened and asked, "How's Chuck?"

"He's okay." My voice trembled with excitement. "He'll be home in a few weeks."

"I hated to hear he got drafted. Man, that's tough. I mean with everything you two have been through. I guess he'll be headed to Nam next."

"If God answers my prayers, he won't."

Kyle cocked his head and smirked. "Oh, he's going. And you might as well get used to the idea. They didn't draft him to stay in the States. They've got the Guard for that."

Saliva flooded my mouth. My throat constricted, making it hard to swallow. I crossed my arms, dug my fingernails into the bare skin, and forced myself to ask, "What's it like…?"

He stared at the ground while several minutes passed. What did he see? "You don't want to know."

His words sent an uncomfortable chill through me. I quickly change the subject. "How long will you be home?"

"I'm pulling out next week. Some buddies and I are meeting up."

"But what about your family? Are you coming back before you have to leave again? Where will you be stationed next?"

The noise of a black GTO drew Kyle's attention. "You better go, Morgan. Maybe I'll catch up with you later."

I slipped my hand in his. "Kyle, I don't understand. What's happened to you?"

He fixed his eyes on mine. "You can't think about it too much and hold on to your sanity. There aren't any answers." He jumped off the table and weaved toward the black car. "I'll be seeing you, Morgan. Tell my buddy to take care."

He got in with the stranger and took off, leaving his car behind.

The parked yellow Camaro brought back pictures of times past—Kyle laughing, sharing stories, even standing beside us the day Chuck and I got married. The car I'd watched leaving the park carried not one, but two, strangers. One of them only looked like someone I once knew.

#

Four weeks later, a light tap on the outside door awakened me.

"What in the world?" I mumbled and peeked at the clock. Six twenty-three. I tossed aside the covers and scooted out of bed, before easing the bedroom curtain back far enough to get a good look at the person on the steps.

"Chuck!" I whirled from the window, knocking the bedside lamp to the floor. It shattered in pieces, but I didn't care. Avoiding pink glass shards, I raced toward another knock.

I swung the door open and lunged for him, wrapping arms around his neck and legs around his waist. "What are you doing here?"

He tossed his duffle bag inside. "Well, I was in hopes my wife still lived here. You are my wife, aren't you? I wasn't able to get a good look at you before being assaulted." He placed his hands on both sides of my face and pressed his lips to mine.

I unwound my legs from his midsection and stood on my toes with our bodies pressed together. "How'd you get here? I thought I was supposed to meet you in Meridian tomorrow night."

"I wanted to surprise you, so I took a bus. Marvin drove to Memphis this morning to get me. But we can talk later."

"Are you hungry?"

"Starving." He scooped me up in his arms, nudged the door closed with his shoulder, and headed for the bedroom. Even with all the crunching beneath his boots, he never took his eyes from mine.

#

The next day, I sat at my desk and stared at the calendar. Several rings of red ink circled today's date. Looking forward to his return, I'd marked off every day since Chuck left for basic training. And here it was, bittersweet. I'd known for two weeks about his new orders. How quick the days would pass before he'd leave again. Yet I spent the afternoon posting debits and credits when I should be home with my husband. My head throbbed. I glanced at my watch. Again. Almost four. Then I remembered the phone call from Chuck's grandmother earlier today. She'd planned a special meal to include the whole family for his first night home. All of his favorites: field peas, turnip greens, cornbread, chicken and dumplings, and banana pudding. I knew he'd enjoy the evening. And why shouldn't he—they were his family, too. But he was my husband, and *I* needed him! Yet here I sat.

I slammed the books closed, grabbed my purse, and stormed up to the sales counter interrupting a sales clerk and customer. "Where's Mr. Latham?"

"Back here, Morgan."

I took long strides, following the clank of metal against metal. "Mr. Latham," I stood facing him, "I can't do this."

He removed a red grease rag from his back pocket and wiped his hands. "Do what?"

"Work. I mean…Chuck's home, and I'm here. In a few weeks he'll be leaving for Vietnam." Just the sound of the word from my lips twisted my emotions to the brink of insanity. "It's not that I don't need this job or appreciate it, but—"

"Hey! Wait a minute." He held up his hand. "I expected you to take time off to be with Chuck. In fact, you didn't have to come in at all today. I would've understood. This place won't fall apart if you're not here every day. Even if the statements go out a week late, so what? Go home. Take the rest of the week off. When you come back Monday, we'll sit down and work out a schedule."

"You mean…?"

"Shoo!" He smiled and waved the back of his hands my direction. "Get out of here. Go be with your husband."

"Thanks," I whispered, unable to say more.

I raced home and pulled in the driveway. Chuck and his two little sisters had set up their Slip And Slide in our side yard. Chuck made a mad dash and belly flopped onto the wet, yellow plastic sheet, sending sprays of water in the air. I laughed as Amy and Beth bowled in on top of him.

He'd always been so easy going, slow to anger, gentle, full of love, and he made life fun. Kyle flashed in my mind. Would Vietnam change all that?

Amy ran to the car, her curly, orange-red, wet hair refusing to lay docile. "Come on. Come play with us."

As I got out of the car, Chuck called, "Go put on your swim suit and help me take some of the starch out of these two."

He sat cross-legged in a pair of cutoff jeans. Water glistened on his tanned, bare chest. How tempting to kick my shoes off and join in their fun on such a hot September day. I'd been so busy hanging on since he left, I'd forgotten how to play. "I would, but we're all supposed to be at your grandmother's for supper in a little over an hour."

"Aww!" he whined, imitating the words and gestures of Amy and Beth. "Let me help these two orangutans pick up this mess. I'll be right in."

After showering and getting dressed, Chuck sat on the couch and pulled me down on his lap. "I know we're running late, but you and I need to talk."

I exhaled. "About what?"

His expression remained serious. "Vietnam. There's no good time to talk about it. But I want to discuss it now, and then try to put it out of our minds for the next four weeks."

I bit down on my bottom lip and nodded.

"There are some things you need to know. The Army provides a GI insurance policy in case something happens—"

I jumped off his lap and waved my hand toward him. "No! I don't want to hear this!"

"You have to. Morgan, listen to me. If I don't make it back—"

"You're coming back!"

Chuck stood and placed his hands on my shoulders. "I promise you, I plan on coming back." He lowered his face within inches of mine. "Do you hear me? But if I don't, you take that money and start a new life. Someplace other than Greer."

I covered my ears. "I'm not listening."

He gently lowered my hands and held me tight. "That's all I wanted you to know. I won't bring it up again. Now let's work on making this the best four weeks we can. We'll spend it making memories."

Too numb to scream, my spirit cried out for God's help. It was all too much to bear. We'd become trapped in an ugly nightmare with no awakening.

"What do you say, Morgan?"

I yank the neck of my shirt up and wiped the tears from my face, then nodded. If Chuck wanted to live the next few weeks with as much normalcy as possible, somehow, I'd make it happen.

Chapter 28

Shades of purple, red, and orange reflected off the clouds in the western sky—the end of another day—and today, the end of another week. Chuck would be leaving next Saturday. My heart raced. My head hurt. I squeezed my eyes shut and willed myself to think only of tonight. We'd invited his little sisters to come over later this evening to roast marshmallows and hotdogs.

Chuck threw another log on the fire. "What's wrong?"

"Nothing. Just admiring the sunset." I sauntered over and handed him two of the four coat hangers to untwist and straighten.

"We can work on these later." He took the potential roasters from my hands and tossed them, along with his, on the blanket next to the fire. "Right now I want to enjoy being with you…alone…in the quietness." He plopped down and tugged my arm.

I snuggled against him, resting my head on his shoulder. "We aren't alone. Our side yard is your grandmother's backyard. And with the size fire you've built, I'm sure we're lit up like the screen at the Skylark Drive-in."

He wrapped his arms around me. His lips pressed against mine, stirring desires meant to be shared by husband and wife.

“I love you, Morgan,” he whispered between kisses.

A gust of wind caught up the smoke, casting it our way. My nose and throat burned, and we stood up coughing. Chuck led me away from its draft and unfolded two lawn chairs. “Are you okay?”

I nodded and rubbed my stinging eyes.

He reached toward the cooler. “Would you like something to drink?”

“Not right now.” I picked up a stick and began poking the coals, sending embers into the soft shade of darkness.

Chuck took a swallow of Coke as he lowered himself in one of the chairs. “Have you ever thought about leaving Mississippi?”

I cringed and hoped he wasn’t building up to what I should do if he didn’t make it back from Vietnam. “No, not really. Why?”

Flickers of light played across his face as he removed the stick from my hand and tossed it in the fire before patting the chair next to his. “How *would* you feel about it if we did… when I get back?”

I looked at him sideways and searched his eyes. “Are you serious?”

“Why not? Think about it. Our parents chose to live in Mississippi. Their parents and their parents’ parents picked Mississippi, but that doesn’t mean we have to stay here. We can go anywhere—Wyoming, Montana, Idaho, Alaska. A guy in basic training spent some time in Idaho. He talked about how beautiful the mountains were and what all there was to do: hunt bear and elk, snowmobile, hike, even whitewater rafting.”

“It’s so far away. We wouldn’t know anybody. How would we decide where to go?”

“That’s the beauty of it. We find out everything we can about each state. It would give us a plan, a sense of direction, something to look forward to. Like when we finally set a date to get married. Remember?”

The thought of planning for the future, rather than living in dread, stirred much-needed hope. "I guess we could go to the library Monday and checkout some books. You know...for the fun of it."

"And if they don't have what we're looking for, we'll find a bookstore that does. But, Morgan, I'm talking actually leaving, finding us a new home. What do you think?"

A smile tugged my lips. "It's wild, crazy, and scary, but I like it."

No sooner had Chuck leaned in for a kiss than a shrill voice pierced the night air. "If you don't wait on me, Amy, I'm telling Mother!"

Chuck pushed from his chair and trotted toward the shadowy forms and voices of his sisters.

#

After church, we gathered at Chuck's grandmother's with family members, including aunts, uncles, and cousins. They all came to tell him good-bye. Difficult, since it should've been a celebration, only hours before his twenty-first birthday. The day stretched long into the evening. Every time someone prepared to leave, I busied myself in the kitchen or escaped to the bathroom to avoid emotional words of departure. My own emotions barely stayed intact. We didn't make it home until well after ten. Then after quick showers, we settled in bed, wrapped in each other's arms. Sleep would be for another time.

Around midnight, I sat straight up.

"Where are you going?"

I swung my legs off the bed and pulled one of his T-shirts over my head. "I'll be right back."

After retrieving a small package from the closet shelf, I hopped back in bed and handed Chuck his gift, wrapped in a paper bag, displaying his two little sisters' artistic abilities. "Happy birthday. It's from me, Amy, and Beth."

"Beth said they drew some pictures for me, but she wasn't supposed to tell." He propped up on his elbow. "I didn't have a clue what she was talking about."

"It's nothing grand, but I wasn't sure what the Army would allow you to have—"

I swallowed and spoke past the lump in my throat. "This way, you'll have all your family with you. And the last page," I flipped to the back cover, "is another masterpiece by Amy and Beth."

"What is it?"

"It's you and me, silly." I poked him in his ribs. "We're fishing. Remember the day we took the girls to Vance Lake?"

"Right." He chuckled. "And Beth and Amy made us paddle from one end to the other, sure the next spot would be where we'd find the bigger fish."

"My arms were sore for three days."

"But we did it…and we'll get through this next year, Morgan. It'll be painful, no doubt about it, but no matter what God has planned for us, we'll paddle our way through life together, with His help."

#

Much too soon, the week closed in on us. I stayed on the verge of tears as we drove to Memphis. The dam broke that night in a hotel room next to the airport, when Chuck took me in his arms and whispered, "I'll miss you."

"How am I going to make it without you? You're everything to me." I sobbed.

"Don't say that. I'm only a man. A man who loves you more

than anyone on this earth ever could, but still a man. God always comes first. Remember that. Don't take your eyes off Him. Ever. He'll get you through the tough times. He'll hold you when I'm not here to hold you, and He'll never let you go. No matter how lonely or afraid you might get, He's your comfort and strength. Tomorrow, I'm leaving you in His hands, and you'll have to give me up to Him, also. And if it's God's will—I pray it is—I'm coming back. I've got too much to live for."

The next morning, we promised each other there'd be no tears when we said our good-byes. A promise I didn't know if I could keep.

As we sat talking and holding hands at the departure gate, I studied Chuck's features, trying to etch each one permanently in my mind: his strong, square chin; the small, faded scar above his left brow; baby blue eyes and ruddy complexion; his callused hands, unafraid of hard work, yet gentle and loving—

"We're now boarding Flight 226 for Denver and Seattle at Gate 13," a woman's voice blasted over the intercom.

My lungs stopped working, I couldn't breathe. I grabbed Chuck's neck and held on. His tears wet the edge of my face; mine absorbed into his uniform.

Only after the last call, did he loosen my grip and cradle my face in his hands. "Look at me, Morgan. In order for us to get our life back, this day had to come. The sooner I get on that airplane, the sooner I'll be back. Read all the books we purchased. I'm counting on you to let me know everything you find out about those states we've talked about. We've got a lot of planning to do in a year. I love you. I've got to go."

He kissed me one last time and headed toward the corridor doorway. Before disappearing from sight, he turned and mouthed, "I love you."

As the agent closed the door behind him, pain gripped my body as though a part of me had been surgically removed. I sat in a daze then walked to the large glass window as the plane taxied toward the runway. Engine vapors and fumes reminded me of a dream, something unreal. But when Chuck's airplane barreled down the runway and left the ground, reality could not be denied.

He was gone.

Chapter 29

In the past, Chuck and I'd made several excursions to Memphis, but he always drove. Once I left the airport parking lot, nothing looked familiar. Which way?

The road signs blurred as silent tears slid down my face, and morning commuters, all fighting for their spot, forced me to go faster than I felt comfortable with. I tightened my grip on the steering wheel and eyed the sign ahead—Interstate 40. After merging with the fast-paced traffic onto the freeway, I took a deep breath and tried to relax. That's when I spotted a huge, metal bridge. I'd gone too far and missed the turn to Interstate 55.

The traffic never really thinned, in fact, the eighteen-wheelers seemed to multiply, their intimidating size sweeping me along to uncomfortable and unaccustomed speeds. Not until I reached the outskirts of West Memphis was I able to pull off the road and stop, climb onto my knees, and retrieve the atlas Chuck had thrown on the backseat "just in case". Forrest City waited forty miles ahead, a halfway spot between Greer and Little Rock, the town where Marsha and Bob lived. I closed my eyes and massaged both temples. The thought of returning to the empty efficiency brought more tears, and my lack of experience driving in yet another big city invoked fear. I'd become so dependent on Chuck, but he wouldn't be around for a year. I put the car in gear and headed farther into Razorback country.

For the next hour, I drove mile after mile along fields with barren cotton stalks, all picked clean of their white fibers. Now ugly and drab, much like the farms at home when only weeks earlier they appeared like blankets of snow that refused to melt under the hot autumn sun. How quickly things changed. Today, uncertainty, separation, and somber times replaced the beauty, joy, and peace Chuck and I shared before the draft. What would tomorrow bring? Given the chance, would I want to know?

I pressed harder on the gas pedal, eager—no desperate—to spend time with Marsha and burying my pain if possible by wrapping myself in the excitement of the unborn life she carried.

#

Ten days after Chuck left, I received my first letter postmarked Vietnam. I tore open the envelope and drank in every word.

Oct. 21st
Dear Morgan,

Remind me never to complain about the rain that we get back home. I've been here two days, but it has rained nonstop. There's nothing but water and mud. It's hot and humid, much like early summer in Mississippi.

The men who've been here awhile are anxious to hear any news from back home. But morale is low with talk of all the war protesting and how our troops are being treated when they return.

I don't know where in Vietnam I'll be stationed yet, so don't try to write me at the return address.

As soon as they assign me, I'll let you know. I miss you so much, babe, and can't wait to hear from you.

By the way, add Colorado to our list. Our plane landed in Denver only briefly, but the Rockies were beautiful from the air. Some of the mountains already had snow.

Tell all the folks hi. Give Amy and Beth a big hug for me. Know that I'm thinking of you and praying for us constantly. I'll write soon. I love you, Morgan.

Forever,
Chuck

I rested my head against the back of the couch and fought to control my tumultuous emotions. Still, one tear slid free. I wiped it away, picked up a pen and stationary, and began to write:

Dear Chuck,

I was so excited to get your letter today. I've been going crazy wondering where you are and how you're doing. Amy and Beth ask about you constantly. By the way, your talk must have helped; your mom's allowing them to spend the night with me this Friday. I'm looking forward to it. They are full of energy and great company.

Good news. Marsha had her baby. Bob called this morning. A girl, eight pounds, four ounces, and seventeen inches long. Gram has her namesake, Rachael Lee. They're planning to come home for Thanksgiving. Of course, Gram and I are thrilled. She can hardly wait to hold her first great-grandchild.

I talked with the librarian Friday and told her about our plans. She's going to research her files to see if she can find more books to help us. I'll add Colorado to our list. It's such an adventure to read about other places and wonder where we'll call home someday.

Got to go. Can't be late for work. I'll add this letter to the others I've written and send them once you give me the word, or I should say address. I sure miss you. I know you'll write when you can. Please be careful. I'm praying for you, also.

Love always,
Morgan

The next morning, I drove over to get Gram. She needed ribbon and buttons to complete the soft, white crocheted cap and sweater she'd been working on for baby Rachael.

At eight forty, there wasn't a cloud in the sky, and the temperature had already reached sixty-eight degrees. The bare deciduous trees made it easy to spot two red squirrels scurrying across the limbs in a game of chase. Many of the neighbors had decorated their porches with harvest scenes of pumpkins, bundles of cornstalks, and scarecrows, resting like men of leisure on bales of hay. I smiled, Gram would enjoy seeing the sights.

After parking under the carport, I got out and petted the gray tabby at my feet before stepping inside. Gram wasn't dressed and waiting in the den, so I headed to her bedroom. She sat on the edge of her bed, still in her pajamas.

I knocked on the doorjamb. "Did you forget about our outing?"

She glanced up. "No, but, darlin', I don't feel up to it today."

I stepped over and placed my hand on her cool forehead. "Are you sick?"

She fluffed her pillow. "I'm fine. I've had breakfast, taken my medicine, and after a couple of hours sleep, I'll feel even better."

"Didn't you sleep well last night?"

She chuckled. "When you get to be my age, between all the aches and pains, not to mention making a half dozen trips to the bathroom, sleeping through the night's a thing of the past." She slipped her shoes off. "I'm fine. Please don't worry about me."

As she pushed herself further back in bed and began to draw up her knees, I leaned down, lifted her legs, and placed them under the covers. Before she turned onto her right side, I noticed a dime-sized, gray-blue area on the outer edge of her cheek. "What's that on your face?"

"Probably dirt or this morning's breakfast. I haven't had a bath. That's another reason I can't go this morning. It'd be time for you to go to work before I could possibly get ready."

"It looks like a bruise. Turn this way so I can take a look."

"Darlin', I'm tired. Bruise, dirt—at my age what difference does it make? It could be most anything." She patted my hand. "Now you run on."

"But how would you have gotten a bruise on your face without knowing?"

She uncovered her left hand. "The same way I got this, who knows. You bump against something without giving it a thought, and the next thing you know, you're wearing five shades of color before the week's out."

She snuggled under the blanket and closed her eyes as if I hadn't remained in the room.

"I'll bring you back something for lunch."

"I may still be in the bed. Why don't you fix me a sandwich and leave it in the refrigerator? I'll eat when I get up. Do you mind closing the curtains? The sun's shining right in my eyes."

Clearly, the conversation was over, but not my concerns. Gram was acting so…I couldn't pick a word to describe her behavior—tired, distant, vague? Something wasn't right.

#

Weeks passed into the beginning of the holidays, and I felt each and every hour of them. Yet Chuck had only been gone a little over a month.

November 25, 1970
Dear Chuck,

You amaze me. The dress you bought for my birthday and hid at your grandmother's was a huge surprise, but now roses for our anniversary? Not only are they beautiful, but the efficiency smells like a wonderful flower garden. Thank you for being so thoughtful.

I hope the chocolate chip cookies made it in time. Know each one was baked and packed with love.

I don't dare think of how you'll spend tomorrow. Neither Thanksgiving, nor our anniversary, will be the same without you. Your grandmother's teaching me how to make fresh cranberry sauce. She says it's one of your favorites, so I'll pay close attention. We'll be saying a special prayer for you and the rest of the men.

Marsha, Bob, and the baby won't be coming home. Rachael Lee's been sick. Nothing serious. Gram and I are very disappointed though. We planned on giving Marsha the quilt we'd made. I mailed it yesterday. Hopefully, we'll see them at Christmas.

Oh, I almost forgot. I'm enclosing the information from the Chamber of Commerce in Cody, Wyoming; Pocatello, Idaho; and Bozeman, Montana. Let me know what you think.

I miss you so much. Happy Anniversary and Thanksgiving, sweetheart. Next year we'll do something special. Of course, just having you back home will be special enough.

Love always,
Morgan

#

The Monday before Christmas, and I hadn't received a letter from Chuck in nine days. He'd warned me there might be times when he wouldn't be able to write. He'd told me I shouldn't worry. Easier said than done. I'd mailed his Christmas package three weeks earlier—everything he'd requested: Kool-Aid, homemade fudge and Martha Washington balls, canned peaches, raisins, gum, baby powder, Q-tips, socks, and razors, along with other miscellaneous items. The simplest things we'd taken for granted, now a luxury.

I sat on the floor untangling a string of lights, listening to the radio as Charley Pride's smooth baritone flooded the little efficiency with "O Holy Night". The scent of the freshly cut cedar, which Chuck's father brought over last night, reminded me of last year's tree that had almost touched the ceiling. The Christmas lights forgotten, I cupped my fingers around the porcelain angel, clothed in white lace, and remembered how Chuck had lifted me so I could place her on top. Suddenly, a new song drew my attention, The Carpenters' "Merry Christmas Darling".

Tears pooled and threatened to overflow. I reached for a Kleenex. Beth and Amy would soon be knocking on the door, ready to help with the decorations. I stood and busied myself warming milk for hot chocolate. The iced sugar cookies had already been placed on a small silver colored tray. Under normal circumstances, the excitement of watching them expel all their pent-up energy would be contagious, but I couldn't squelch the uneasy feelings.

God, I need to know he's okay. Please watch over him.

By the Monday after New Year's, I still hadn't received a letter from Chuck, and every reasonable explanation no longer sounded feasible. I'd burned two pieces of toast and knocked over a glass of orange juice. I wouldn't be able to function if I didn't talk to someone, so I pulled on my navy pea coat and headed to see Gram. My stomach rolled with waves of nausea as worries ran rampant. Seeing Mom's car parked in the driveway didn't help. Maybe she and Dad rode together.

I got out of the car, took several deep breaths of the cool winter air, and walked to the side door. After getting no response to my knock, I let myself in and started down the hallway toward Gram's room.

Mom's voice halted my progress. "I'm sick and tired of all this whining and complaining. You don't do anything but sit around this house all day and think up another ailment. What did Doctor Banks find wrong three months ago? Nothing! Attention's all you're after."

I eased into the room. Gram sat on the bed with Mom towering over her. Soft sobs escaped through the wrinkled hands covering her face.

"And another thing, I've had enough of this crying. Stop it!"

"Leave her alone!" I blurted, scooting past Mom.

Gram fell against my chest weeping as I placed an arm around her shoulder.

Mom glared at me, then pointed at the door. "You get yourself out of this house, now!"

"Not until I find out what's going on."

"You'll leave, or I'll call your father."

A familiar twinge ran through me. I swallowed hard, but held myself up straight and stared her down. "Call him. Because I'm not leaving."

She drew her hand back. "Why you—"

I moved away from Gram. "Go ahead! Maybe then your mother will see this has nothing to do with her…it's you. Why couldn't I see it before now? All the years I spent trying to make you love me, to make you proud of me, but that wasn't possible, because it never was about me. Was it?"

Mom stood there, her hand frozen in midair, her face flushed.

"Why won't you answer me?"

Her hand lowered. Her chest rose and fell at fast intervals as if she were short of breath. "We'll see how much you run that mouth of yours once your father gets here." She whirled on her heel and stomped out of the room.

Gently pulling Gram's hands from her face, I crouched and peered straight into her eyes. "We've got to get you out of here."

She didn't budge.

Crossing the width of the room, I opened the closet, grabbed her suitcase from the top shelf, and laid it on the foot of the bed. After unlatching the lid, I snatched her clothes off the hangers and tossed them inside. At the dresser, I gathered an armload of undergarments and threw them in. "Is this all of your medicine?" I gestured to the array of different drugs. But again, she didn't respond. I reached back inside the closet, dumped a pair of shoes from their box, and swept the bottles inside.

"What do you think you're doing?"

Mom's voice startled me. I spun sideways in time to see her hurl Gram's luggage to the floor.

"Mother's not going anywhere."

Dad could arrive any minute. Panic threatened to overrule my judgment. Physically I'd be no match. I slid the shoebox under my arm and thrust my hand through the straps of Gram's purse. I gently tugged her forward and up. "Come on. We're leaving. We'll get your things another time."

Without a word, she stood and allowed me to lead her out of the room. We made it halfway down the hall before Mom jerked Gram out of my grasp. "I said you're not taking her! If you try to take her out of this house, I'll call the police!"

As though my hearing diminished, I could no longer make out the words of her rant. I wrapped my arm around Gram and focused on getting her out the door and inside the car. Once Gram lowered herself in the passenger seat, I locked her door and ran to the other side, got in, and started the engine.

"Open this door!" Mom beat on the passenger window until I backed the car out the driveway.

Minutes later, Dad passed me, speeding toward the house. Would the police soon follow? In less than forty minutes, we reached Danville where I took Interstate 55 south. It would take an hour to make it to Gram's—the house I'd always loved as a child. Would the highway patrol be looking for us? What would happen if Gram couldn't convince them she was mentally capable of making her own decisions? She'd not said a word since we left Greer. *God, I don't know what to do.*

"Gram, I'm going to take the next exit and find a phone."

"I'm glad Henry didn't live to see how Dot treated me." Gram began crying again. "Your grandfather thought the world of her."

I read the road sign ahead—Enid 10 miles—and remembered the little store, close to the cabin where Chuck and I'd spent our honeymoon. They'd have a payphone. Memories of our special weekend, now so long ago, mingled with my ever-present fears over our broken communications. *Where are you, Chuck?*

Gravel crunched beneath the tires as I stopped feet from the bait shop's front entrance. There were no payphones outside.

"Gram, I'll be right back. I'm going to lock the car. Don't open the door for anyone."

I ran inside, scanned the walls, and spotted a black phone hanging behind the man at the counter. "Please, I need to make a collect call. I'll pay you."

He nodded, without saying a word.

My insides shook like Jell-O. So did my hands. I could scarcely dial zero.

Marsha answered on the third ring and accepted the charges. "Morgan, what's wrong?"

Hearing my sister's voice released a new flood of tears. "It's Gram. I couldn't leave her—"

"Leave her where? What are you talking about?"

I turned my back to the man, cupped the mouthpiece, and briefly explained the morning's events. "I'd first planned on taking her to her house, but Mom threatened to call the police. For all I know, they might not let her stay in her own home. I don't know what to do or where to take her."

"Where are you now?"

"Close to Enid Lake."

"First of all, don't get back on the interstate. Find 82 and stay on it all the way to Memphis. You're going to take her to Uncle Frank's. He's always wanted her, but Mom wouldn't allow it. When we hang up, I'll call and tell him everything."

"I'm not sure how to get to his house."

"You know where the Southaven Mall is, right before you get to Memphis?"

"Yes."

"He'll meet you at the main entrance."

"How do you know? What if you can't get in touch with him?"

"Don't worry. I'll find him. If not, Aunt Sally will meet you. Everything's going to be fine. You did the right thing. Gram can't stay with our parents. They broke us, but at least we had hope that someday we'd get out. They'll destroy her if she stays with them. If they haven't already. After I get in touch with Uncle Frank, I'll head that way. We'll talk more tonight."

"Marsha—" My voice cracked. I swallowed hard. "I haven't heard from Chuck in over three weeks. What do you think that means?"

Always the big sister—reassuring, calm, never at a loss for words—Marsha didn't respond. With each second of silence, my heart rate raced out of control. "I've got to go. See you tonight."

I hung up the phone. *Can You see me, God? Can You hear me?*

Without making eye contact, I held out a dollar bill and some change, but the storeowner pushed my hand away and wished me luck.

I got back in the car and cradled Gram's arthritic hands in mine. She looked at me for the first time since we left Mom's. Her pale blue irises, surrounded by streaks of red and pools of tears reminded me of a frightened animal—they reminded me of my own reflections in years past.

"It's going to be all right, Gram. We're going to be fine."

Chapter 30

From the moment Gram laid eyes on Uncle Frank, it was as if she became the child and he the nurturing parent. Her sobs turned into wails when he lifted her from my car and cradled her in his arms. She clung to his hand, even after Aunt Sally and I got her in bed. He didn't ask any questions, only smiled and assured her he'd stay until she fell asleep.

Marsha had made the right decision. Gram was safe and where she belonged.

Later that afternoon, Marsha, with baby Rachael, and I sat at the kitchen table with our uncle. The evening sun poured through the bay window. Its warmth did little to chase away the chill as we expressed our suspicions regarding Gram's mistreatment and shared details about the cruelty of our childhood.

Aunt Sally set the tray next to the kitchen sink. "She drank part of her milk, but I couldn't get her to eat a bite."

Who could blame her? The thought of food turned my own stomach.

Uncle Frank's chair scraped against the floor as he pushed himself from the table. "Give it here. Let me see what I can do."

"No." Aunt Sally placed her hand on his. "You'll only upset

her. You're too angry right now, and it shows."

"I'm not angry at her. It's that…that…"

"Misguided sister of yours," she finished his statement.

"Not exactly the words I had in mind." He glanced at Marsha and me. "And I'm telling all of you right now, this isn't over. Dot won't get by with this, and she wouldn't have gotten by with mistreating you children had I known what was going on in that house. I wish you two would have come to me, told me before today."

"It wouldn't have done any good." Marsha pulled the partially empty bottle from baby Rachael's mouth and placed her over her right shoulder. "We told plenty of people." She glanced at me. "At least I did. Schoolteachers, the preacher, other adults in the town. Morgan even went to see a lawyer. None of them did a thing. I guess because what the lawyer told Morgan was true: The law wasn't on our side."

He frowned. "Well, he was either a moron or he thought you were talking about a mere spanking."

"No, sir," I spoke up. "When he said he needed proof, I let him know I was wearing the proof and what it looked like. That's when he tried to explain the law and told me if I pursued his help, and *if* things were truly as bad as I said, it would only make matters worse for me. He. Knew."

Uncle Frank's face paled. "Then he *was* an idiot. There are agencies in this country designed to protect children. And Memphis has some fine lawyers who would have made sure your *parents* understood the law. And as for Chuck, first thing in the morning we'll contact the local Red Cross, even though I'm sure he's fine. In fact, you'll probably find a letter in the mail tomorrow when we go back after yours and Mamma's things. I don't want you staying in Greer, especially now. You're better off here with us."

"I can't."

"Why not!" Little Rachael jumped at Marsha's sharp words.

"Because I have a job for one thing—unless he decides to fire me for not showing up today."

"You called him. Besides, let him fire you," Marsha ranted. "If that's the only thing keeping you there, then I hope he does."

"She's right, Morgan." Aunt Sally used a much calmer approach. "You don't need to be there by yourself."

They didn't understand. They didn't have Chuck's word's, "If something happens to me, I want you to start a new life, someplace besides Greer", playing over and over in their mind. For me, leaving would be like admitting he was not coming back.

"When Chuck comes home, he'll expect to find me in Greer."

Marsha's scowl deepened. "Don't be a fool, Morgan. He'd be the first one to tell you to get out of there after what's happened with Gram."

"What Mom and Dad say and do aren't nearly as important as finding Chuck. Besides, his parents don't have a clue that I haven't heard from him in weeks. When I explain everything that's happened, his father won't let anything happen to me."

Marsha's eyebrows shot up. Her lips pinched tight.

"He won't," I stated with conviction.

"Will you at least think about it? And when—not if—Mom and Dad start in on you, will you promise me you'll leave?"

"If it gets that bad, yes."

#

Aunt Sally gave Marsha and me one of the downstairs bedrooms across the hall from Gram's. Rachael Lee slept soundly between us as we talked, neither of us able to give in to sleep.

"Do you suppose Uncle Frank's right about the Red Cross

helping me find Chuck?"

"He ought to know. He was in the Navy during WWII. I'm sure he saw firsthand what they're capable of, but I also think he's right about Chuck being fine. You worry too much."

"What do you think he'll say to Mom when he sees her tomorrow?"

"I don't know." Marsha sat up and placed her pillow between her back and the headboard. "It won't be pretty. I can guarantee that. I'd give anything to hear it though. It'll be the first time anyone's stood up to her and called her what she is…an abuser."

"What do you think Dad will do?"

"To Uncle Frank?" She huffed. "Nothing if he's smart."

"Do you suppose—"

"Shhhh." Marsha hushed me and then lunged out of bed.

"What is it?"

"Gram." Marsha headed for the door. "Sounds like she's crying. Stay with Rachael."

"I'm coming, too."

"No," she ordered. "Stay with the baby."

I turned on the closet light and grabbed pillows to brace Rachael, so I could stand in the doorway and listen. When I heard Marsha say, "Let me get Morgan", I went to the closet and pulled blankets from the shelf and began making a pallet, then gently laid Rachael on the floor.

As we helped her to the bathroom and out of her soiled clothes, tears ran along ruts time etched into Gram's face. "I hate you girls have to see me in such a mess."

"You did the same for us plenty of times," Marsha assured her.

"Dot'll have a fit about the bed."

"You're not in Greer," I reminded her. "You're at Uncle Frank's and Aunt Sally's, remember?"

She sat on the toilet and stared off in space. "Henry spoiled Dot. Gave her everything she ever wanted, right up until the day he died. I'm glad he didn't see…"

Gram didn't finish her thought. She didn't have to. She said it earlier in the car.

#

"Morgan." A warm hand pressed against my right shoulder.

I sat straight up, and like Gram, for a moment lost my bearings.

Aunt Sally stood over me. "Was the baby fussy last night?"

"I don't guess so." I rubbed the sleep from my eyes.

"Then why are you out here on the couch?"

"Oh, that." I tried to focus on the mantle clock. "Good thing you left us a choice of gowns and pajamas. Gram had an accident, so we put her in bed with Marsha and Rachael. Her sheets and gown are in the washing machine."

"We need to get a move on, Morgan." Uncle Frank stood in the doorway. Steam rose from the white mug he held. "We've got a full day ahead of us."

"You just settle yourself down, Frank Collins. It'll be another two hours before the Red Cross opens. Besides, before you make a trip to Greer, you need to talk to your mamma and see what she wants to do."

"There's *no way* she's going back to Dot's. *Nobody's* going to mistreat my mamma. I've put up with a lot from my sister through the years. Jay and I used to get our butts beat on a regular basis. All she'd have to do was tell Daddy some sad tale—the truth or a downright lie—throw in a few tears for good measure, and he'd take a belt to us. My old man thought she could do no wrong. Well, this time it's my mamma, and I won't keep my mouth shut any longer."

Déjà vu? No. Even though I'd never heard the story before, I could see it and feel it as if I'd lived in his very skin. "Did she watch?"

"What?" He shifted and leaned against the doorframe.

"When Granddaddy took off his belt and whipped you and Uncle Jay, did she watch?"

"She certainly did. And grinned like a Cheshire cat. Why she'd..."

His voice faded. Yet it all became so clear. For some sick reason, the need to watch, be the one to control the timing and amount of the inflicted pain on someone else started as a child and grew worse with age. Had she become like a drug addict, who needed more and more in order to obtain the same high as at first? But on the other hand, it didn't make sense. How did she pull Dad into her game?

Chapter 31

"Ready?" Uncle Frank asked as he turned the knob to the door clearly marked Red Cross.

Just seeing the bold red letters and the red cross—their emblem that looked more like a plus sign than a cross—gave me hope and peace of mind. Finally, someone who'd help me find Chuck. Then without warning, optimism faded with the niggling question, "but what if"?

I shook my head, refusing to allow Satan's tormenting to take root, and smiled at my uncle. "Yes, sir."

Inside, posters—portraying nurses dressed in uniforms of days long ago, military men from all branches, and young families in need—papered the walls.

"Can I help you?" An attractive woman, whose jet-black hair didn't match her gray streaked roots, approached and introduced herself.

"We're counting on it." My uncle gave a confident nod. "My niece," he placed a hand on my shoulder, "needs your help locating her husband. He's stationed in Vietnam, and she hasn't heard from him for several weeks now."

"Please," she motioned toward chairs across from a nearby

metal desk, "have a seat." Once we all settled, she picked up a pen and rolled it between her palms. "It's not unusual to have a lull between letters, Mrs.—I'm sorry, I didn't get your name."

"Mathews. Morgan Mathews."

"As I was saying, it's not unusual to have a lull between letters—"

"But he writes to me almost every day." I wanted to still her hands, stop the pen from clicking against her rings. "I've received at least one letter, sometimes two, every week since he's been there."

"Perhaps he does try, but if he's away from his base camp and out on mission, it may not always be possible. And no matter what he may have written, he couldn't mail it until he got back in camp. It would then most likely be shipped to one of the larger cities like Da Nang before being bagged and flown to the States. So you see, unfortunately the mail service can be slow."

"You don't get it. I know." I patted my chest. "Everything inside me knows something's not right."

The chair squeaked in protest under the weight of the woman whose name I'd already forgotten. "Sometimes I think it's harder on the ones at home than our loved ones over there." She leaned forward, propping on her elbows. "What I'm about to say may sound harsh, but I certainly don't mean for it to be. If your husband had been injured, or God forbid killed, you would have been contacted rather quickly. The old saying 'no news is good news' may be tough to accept, but it's very true in times of war."

"Not that what you've said doesn't make good sense," Uncle Frank spoke up, "but is there nothing you can do?"

She smiled and shifted her gazed back to me. "Exactly when did you last hear from your husband?"

"The twelfth of December."

Her eyes focused on the desk calendar. "Have you received any of your letters or packages back?"

"No, ma'am."

"I'm assuming you sent a Christmas package?"

"Yes, ma'am."

"Well there you have it." Her smile broadened. "You have nothing to worry about. I'm sure your husband's next letter is probably already on its way with a perfectly reasonable explanation for why he hasn't written sooner."

"So you won't help me locate him?" My voice trembled.

"Mrs. Mathews, if we contacted every company commander every time a wife or mother failed to hear from their husband or child within what they deemed a reasonable timeframe, they wouldn't be able to spend their time wisely, protecting their men and fighting this war. Nor would they take the Red Cross seriously. I'm sorry."

Uncle Frank stood and held out his hand. "Thank you for your time."

Once again, she assured me I had nothing to worry about. Empty words did nothing to calm the panic festering inside me.

She handed me her card. "If I can be of further assistance, don't hesitate to call."

I wanted to ask, "How much time would have to pass without hearing from Chuck before you'll help?" Instead, I dropped the card inside my purse, thanked her, and headed for the door, refusing to give in to the tears begging for release.

#

I followed Uncle Frank to Mom's and helped him pack Gram's things, then went by the efficiency to change clothes and on to the parts house with minutes to spare.

Mr. Latham didn't ask for an explanation for my absence yesterday, but I gave him one all the same. Like Uncle Frank, he assured me, "Why, I bet next time you check your mailbox, they'll be one—no, probably two or three of them—waiting on you."

But today's mail had already run, and once again, the mailbox set empty.

I made him promise not to tell anyone. Pity and undue sympathy would only stir up a whole bag of emotions better left tied up.

The part about Gram would be something I'd only share with Chuck's Father. Mom would have to say something in her own defense to Uncle Frank and anyone in the town who learned Gram no longer lived with her. Her version of what happened didn't matter. Gram was safe.

#

I closed the mailbox. Its emptiness resembling the void in my life without Chuck and Gram. Four days since I'd talked with the lady from Red Cross, and still nothing.

A shrill ring called from inside the efficiency. My heart galloped, matching my feet's pace as I ran into the house.

"Hello," I panted, mostly due to nervousness rather than the jog.

Rachael's wailing made it difficult to hear Marsha's words. "Have you heard anything from Chuck?"

"No, not a word, and this waiting is about to drive me nuts. Sounds like I'm not the only one in a bad mood. What's the matter with her this morning?"

The crying stopped.

"Hungry! But everything's under control now. I switched arms and didn't get the bottle plugged in fast enough."

I got tickled. "So you've finally met your match."

"We don't really argue, I give her what she wants, when she wants it, and we get along fine. And speaking of getting along…what's been happening between you and our parents?"

"Haven't seen them. But then all I do is work and come home. Now that Gram's in Memphis, my days are even longer and lonelier. I sure miss her."

Marsha cleared her throat. "She's one of the reasons I called."

"Why? What's wrong?"

"You know Aunt Sally talked about taking her to see a doctor."

"Yeah…"

"She did, and he did some X-rays and blood work. They don't know for sure what's wrong, but she has an appointment to see a specialist."

"A specialist? For what?"

"Her white count is high. Real high. They're thinking leukemia."

I slid down the wall until my bottom rested on the floor. "Cancer? Does Gram know?"

"Uncle Frank doesn't want to tell her until they know for sure."

The vision of Mom standing over Gram, shouting, "I'm sick and tired of all this whining and complaining. You don't do anything but sit around this house all day and think up another ailment", popped in my head. "She knows. Gram knows."

Chapter 32

Each day I trod the worn path to the mailbox. Each day my heart grew heavier, my prayers longer, and my patience shorter. Over four weeks, and still no word from Chuck.

My suitcase waited beside the door packed and ready to be loaded in the car. Gram's diagnosis of Leukemia had not become official, but in my heart, I knew we wouldn't have her much longer.

Chuck's Dad pulled up beside me and stopped. "Anything?"

"Nothing."

He rested his hands on the steering wheel and stared toward the roadside, worry lines etched between his eyes.

"Did you write his company commander like I suggested?"

"It went out yesterday."

"Good. Maybe that'll get us some answers. Meanwhile, don't give up hope, Morgan."

"Never," I forced a smile and assured him. And I wasn't about to.

"You headed to Memphis?"

"Yes, sir. Since I worked a full day yesterday, Mr. Latham gave me today—Look!" I pointed at Mr. Stewart's black Toyota pickup as it turned onto our road.

"Well, I be dog. Fred's running late today."

Fred made his way from mailbox to mailbox before stopping in front of mine.

"Fred." Mr. Mathews nodded. "Hope you've got a letter from my boy somewhere in that stack of junk mail you carry around with you."

"As a matter of fact." Mr. Stewart sported a wide grin as he held up a white envelope.

I drew in a deep breath and reached for the letter, my hands itching to touch it, my eyes burning to see Chuck's handwriting and to know he was okay.

Mr. Mathews and Mr. Stewart exchanged pleasantries as I ripped open the envelope. Hands shaking, I scanned the single page for an explanation on his not writing while aching to know he was truly all right. Later, in private, I'd savor each one of his words.

"Well?" Mr. Mathews asked.

The words *hospital* and *Malaria* jumped off the page. My hand clutched the neck of my sweater. "He's been sick."

"What kind of sick?"

"He says, 'I'm sorry for not writing sooner, but somehow, in spite of the medication the Army issued to prevent malaria, I ended up with it. It seems I'm not the only one. The hospital here in Long Ben has several of us. Some had it much worse than me. Try not to worry. The worst is over. They're talking about shipping me back to base camp. Exactly when, I'm not sure. As soon as I know more, I'll write. Let the folks know I'm okay. Looking forward to'..." I glanced at Mr. Mathews, my face growing warm. "The rest is kind of personal."

He hooted and readjusted his hat. "Good! Now I *know* he's doing better." The sparkle of mischief lit up his eyes. "Now you and his mother can stop your frettin'."

The thought of Chuck having malaria, a disease I knew nothing about, scared me. But my heart was grateful to God for answering my prayers. Yet, until Chuck returned home safely, I'd never stop "frettin'."

#

January 25 and the rush was on to get Chuck's homemade box of Valentine goodies mailed, but first I had to decide which of the three cards in my hand to purchase. I glanced at my watch then reread, for the third time, the last one I'd picked out.

"How could you do something so unspeakable?" My mother's voiced hissed next to my ear.

My purse straps slipped from my shoulder to my wrist, knocking the cards and envelopes to the floor.

"I've never been so embarrassed in my life," she muttered. "You'll never change."

I hoisted my purse to my left shoulder while eyeing the sprawled mess on the floor, making no attempt to pick it up.

"Not. Ever." Venom laced each word.

Still, I said nothing.

She stepped closer. "Because of your lies, I've been over here sorting through copies of the past years' statements. Seems my brother and his wife questioned some of the drugs Mother takes, and at the same time, they enquired about why her bill and mine are not kept separate. Insinuated I used Mother's money to pay for my personal use. I guess I'm no longer responsible for paying her bills. In fact," she spoke through clenched teeth, "I've been advised, by my brother I'm no longer on Mother's bank account."

"She's sick."

"Mother's always sick." She smirked.

"Didn't Uncle Frank tell you? Gram has Leukemia."

"Hum!" She crossed her arms. "I *bet* she does."

"Why would he make something like that up?"

"You mean lie?" Her voice rose an octave. "You're asking me why someone would lie? You *are* pitiful."

"The doctor gives her only six months."

Her eyes narrowed. Her mouth twisted. "And I give my brother and his wife two before they drag her back here for me to take care of."

I locked eyes with her. Had she ever loved Gram? Any of us?

#

I marked through the date, March 10, before turning off the lights and crawling in bed. Another day closer to Chuck's return. Joy and hope mixed with sadness, because it also meant another day closer to losing Gram. She looked so pale, so tired when I told her good-bye Monday. Marsha said she'd given up.

#

April 14, 1971
Dear Chuck,

It's almost seven a.m. Just got off the phone with Aunt Sally. Gram's gone. Aunt Sally said she died suddenly and without suffering. I hope so. She suffered enough already.

I wish I'd spent more time with her. But Marsha and I both take comfort in knowing she was loved and cared for by Uncle Frank and Aunt Sally and surrounded by their grown children and families for the past four months. We only wish she had been with them all along.

I will always blame myself for not seeing the signs earlier. For not protecting her.

Please take care of yourself. I miss you so much.

Love always,
Morgan

#

Bob, Marsha—holding Gram's little namesake—and I walked up the cracked narrow sidewalk to Gram's house where her body lay as she'd requested. Daffodils, pink hyacinths, and purple irises sprang through layers of dead grass and leaves in the front beds. Unpruned yellow bells had almost taken over the side yard. A piece of molding was missing from one of the large, tapered white columns supporting the wraparound porch we'd played on and under as kids. As we reached the front door, in my mind I could still see garlands outlining the massive wooden door, as the red bells hung against its etched glass center, their blinking lights greeting us every Christmas Eve from years past.

"There they are," Mom announced as we stepped inside. She rushed through the crowd of family and others paying their respects, her arms extended. "It's about time."

Marsha and I glanced at one another. My sister's eyes widened. Her mouth flew open in silence.

I backed away, trying to make sense of our mom's peculiar behavior. But when she reached for Rachael and cooed, "Come here to me", it all made sense. She played the role of the doting grandmother well.

Rachael clung to Marsha's neck and began to wail.

Mom recoiled and huffed, "What's the matter? Is she sick?"

Marsha hugged Rachael close and rocked while whispering softly against her ear, "It's okay. You're okay, now."

"She's been a little fussy," Bob responded. "She's getting her first tooth."

My sister's calming whispers stopped as she gave her husband a scathing look. "She's not fussy. She's scared."

"What's going on?" Dad approached, his gaze shifting between

Marsha and me.

Mom lifted her chin and glared at Marsha. I suspected feeling more sure of herself with Dad at her side. "Spoiled is more like it."

"You really want to go there?"

I held my breath at Marsha's words. She'd never back down from either of them again.

Without another word, Mom whirled and retreated.

"I didn't think so." Marsha then turned to Bob. "Would you mind getting the diaper bag out of the car? Rachael needs changing, and she's hungry, I'm sure."

"I'll go," I insisted.

Dad walked out behind me, but said nothing until I'd made it back up the steps with bag in hand. "We need to talk," he demanded and didn't wait for a reply. "The problems you've caused between your mother and her brother were unnecessary and uncalled for."

What did he expect me to say? Obviously not the truth.

"Do you realize that could be your mother lying in there?" He nodded toward the house.

"But it's not. It's Gram."

"When I die," he stuck his finger in my face, "so help me God, if you so much as shed one tear, I'll roll over in my grave."

At that very instant, the depth of Dad's hate and contempt for me sunk in. Then just as quickly, Chuck's face came to mind. I knew love—what it looked like and what it felt like. And this wasn't it. For the first time in my life, I really studied my dad's eyes and saw the man behind them.

I had more than five months to go without Chuck by my side to protect me. But somewhere along the way I'd found courage. And courage came with a price. There was no winning, only accepting what had to be.

"Good-bye, Daddy." No longer afraid, my heart ached as I walked past him.

God, help me to forgive them both.

Chapter 33

With each announcement of arrivals and departures, I pulled my attention from the Life Magazine in my hands and listened carefully. I'd arrived two hours earlier, too excited to wait anywhere but here...the place Chuck and I said our last good-byes.

"Family or friend?" the thin elderly woman sitting next to me asked.

"My husband," I eagerly announced.

"Oh my." Her smile widened. "You don't look old enough to be married."

"It'll be three years in two months."

"Any children?"

"No, ma'am. Not yet."

"Well, you're young. There's still time."

Time? Mine and Chuck's life had been put on hold for the past eighteen months, thanks to the Army. And if not for troop withdrawal that actually began in 1970, he would've been another thirty-three days in Vietnam.

"Today I finally get to meet my first great grandbaby. I'm told she looks a great deal like me. Poor thing." She swallowed a deep raspy giggle. "Of course, I've been told I was quiet the looker in my time."

I could see it, her flawless rosy complexion, beautiful smile, doe eyes. "You still are."

Her face flushed. "I wasn't fishing for a compliment. Really. Simply repeating what my husband used to say. Has your husband been gone long?"

Seems like forever. "I haven't seen him for three-hundred and thirty-three days."

She cocked her head sideways. "Goodness!"

"He's been in Vietnam."

"Oh!"

"Ladies and gentlemen, may I have your attention please?"

I took a deep breath hoping…praying Chuck's flight had not been delayed.

"There it is!" The woman sitting next to me pointed toward the wide glass window to the left.

People crowded around a narrow roped off area as soon as the attendant opened the corridor door.

The elderly woman gathered up her purse and sweater. "Good luck to you and your husband."

"Thank you." I watched as she joined others trying to get the first glimpse of their loved ones.

My heart galloped. My lungs couldn't keep up with its pace. This was it. Would he still feel the same way about me? His letters said so. But there were so many things his letters didn't say. Not one time had he shared the horror of taking a life or the fear and close calls of losing his. Kyle in the park flashed into my mind. His lifeless eyes. His lack of desire to be around family and friends.

The chatter of voices, along with squeals and laughter, increased. I stood on my tiptoes but still couldn't make out more than the top of someone's head. I worked my way out of the waiting area and moved to a clearing several feet away. People pushed in front of me, crowding in, making it difficult to see everyone who passed by.

Then I saw him. "Chuck!" I fought my way upstream, against the flow of people, trying to find him again.

A hand snagged mine, pulling me forward until I stood studying the face I'd etched in my mine almost a year earlier. Only this time his complexion was more tanned. And tiny lines outlined the outer edges of his eyes…his bright eyes that danced with life as he smiled and took me in his arms.

"I've missed you." The warmth of his breath against my ear sent longing chills through my body.

I rested my head against his chest and, for the first time in almost a year, completely relaxed. He'd made it. I'd made it. And when he captured my lips with his, there was no doubt, *we'd* made it.

Epilogue

After Chuck completed his two-year stint with the Army, he and I pursued our dream. We left the Mississippi Delta and headed west. The beauty of the Rockies near Colorado Springs, with their sculptured peaks and pristine water, pushed us onward, as it must have early explorers, eager to see what lay ahead. The bear, elk, and moose of Yellowstone walked fearlessly, allowing us to admire their strength and beauty. Chugwater, Wyoming gave us our first taste of trout and the best cherry pie we'd ever eaten. Montana skies offered more stars than we'd ever imagined existed. Mount Rushmore proved dreams can come true. But after touring twenty-two states, God led us to Lewiston, Idaho. The place we now call home.

THE END

A Note from the Author

Thank you for choosing Hidden Scars. Abuse is an ugly word, which knows no boundaries. Often the victim is left with physical and emotional scars that can only heal with time and by God's love. The why questions may never be answered. Our inability to change the past or to know if there'll be a tomorrow is the reality we must face. When we hang on to the past and refuse to accept God's help with forgiveness, we continue to allow the abuser to inflict pain, even if from the grave. Forgiveness doesn't come easy or overnight, and it doesn't always mean forgetting, but with God, all things are possible. So rather than dwelling on what might have been if loved by a parent, a spouse, a child, or mankind as a whole, be reminded of the people God placed in your life who love you for who you are.

I'd love to hear from you. A review on the site where you purchased the book would be extremely helpful, or you can visit me at my website, amandasueking.com.

Sincerely,
Amanda King

Acknowledgments

Hidden Scars might have remained tucked away in my computer, in its very rough form, if not for my sister, Marion. Your persistence helped me have the courage to take that first giant step.

To all my writer friends and family whose input kept me humble and the story moving forward with purpose, thank you—B. Noyes, N. Kimball, K. Freeman, C. Regnier, B. Steury, F. Lamb, D. Dulworth, K. Broomes, G. Engel, T. Wainwright, A. Trent, D. Zellman., B. Lowe, J. Foster

And to my editor and coach, from Brilliant Cut Editing, I will forever be grateful to God for bringing you into my life. What a blessing you've been. Your wisdom, patience, drive, and faith amaze me.

My husband and best friend, when you said early in our marriage that we'd pull this wagon together, you truly meant it. I couldn't have written this book without you.

About the author

A native of Mississippi, Amanda and her husband—childhood sweethearts—now reside in the Appalachian mountains of Tennessee.

At the age of eleven, Amanda decided someday she'd be a nurse. A career that not only allowed her to help others, but also introduced her to people whose strength and courage, lives and deaths—and faith—would forever change her.

Some of her favorite things are: chocolate anything, antique dishes, new socks, quiet times with her husband, reading a good book, and making people laugh.

Amanda describes herself as loyal, simple, and country through-and-through. She never tires of her peaceful, safe lifestyle or playing with all the newborn farm animals. Even most of her chickens have names.

Check Out The Latest Book by this Author

After four years of begging God to heal her mother, twenty-two-year-old MAMIE CARLSON stands numb as the casket lowers into the grave. Angry with God and fed up with her alcoholic father's depravity and infidelity, Mamie drives away from the cemetery and the Mississippi Delta. Never again will she ask God for anything, and never will a man own a piece of her heart.

The next morning, long before sunup, a waitress offers Mamie more than a free cup of coffee. She paints a picture of a quaint Ozark town less than an hour away and then flips a coin.

In hopes of finding a peaceful life, Mamie accepts the waitress's challenge and soon finds herself aboard a ferry crossing Norfork Lake, for Mountain Home, Arkansas.

When a dirt-layered, five-year-old tyke waltzes uninvited into Mamie's life, she becomes entangled in a web of abuse. She's no match for the abuser. Battered and afraid, Mamie accepts a man, QUINN RAGLAND's protection. Then the unthinkable happens, he confesses deepening feelings for her. Now Mamie must face her worst fear…love.

Made in the USA
Columbia, SC
07 May 2020